TUG OF WAR

TUG OF WAR

JOE RICHARDS

David McKay Company, Inc.
New York

Portions of Chapters 1, 2, 3, 4, 5, and 6 have previously appeared in the March 1968, April 1968, July 1968, September 1968, April 1969, and May 1970 issues of *The Skipper*.

Library of Congress Cataloging in Publication Data

Richards, Joe, 1933-
Tug of war.

1. Sea stories. I. Title.
PZ7.R5156Tu   [PS3568.I3154]   813'.5'4   78-26470
ISBN 0-679-51351-5

10 9 8 7 6 5 4 3 2 1

MANUFACTURED IN THE UNITED STATES OF AMERICA

TUG OF WAR

1

Running the long, lonely stretches of the Intracoastal Water-way in *Princess,* my Friendship sloop, I often wondered what it would be like to make the passage in style.

Like with a full crew, a good cook, somebody to help keep the vessel going while I slept, work her off the mud flats when she ran aground, tie her up sensibly when she docked, keep her clean, provisioned, operational. Forget it.

That takes loot. More loot than I could dream of getting my hands on without a gun and a bandanna over my face.

Of course if I had a rich uncle with his will in order and a coronary occlusion coming up, maybe I could spook him and bring things to a head. I didn't have an uncle. Even a poor one. I did have *Princess.*

Suddenly I had an uncle. That uncle was plenty spooked on the seventh day of December in the year 1941. He damn near had an occlusion. That's how I got to sail on the ST49 complete with captain, crew, cook, and the wherewithal to run her all the way down the inside ditch and out to sea.

I was a deckhand on the ST49, a small tug that belonged to the Army, She was built to haul barges of oil up the coast. Inside. Out of range of the Nazi torpedoes.

A lot of ships were lost. Gradually the torpedoes grew scarce. The big new oil tankers, protected by a growing Air Force and an expanding Navy, were doing better. There was nothing for a small tug to do. That's when the order came to send them off to war. Some were earmarked to cross the Atlantic and join the armada on D-Day. The ST49 was headed for the Pacific down Chesapeake Bay. For a vessel as tender as the ST49, the open ocean would be nothing but hell and damnation. This part was heaven.

The watches were set in Chesapeake City in the expectation of an orderly passage down the Intracoastal Waterway. It was four on and eight off. The eight off was a fat slice of bliss.

I lay in my bunk till noon watching the Chesapeake go by the door. I watched the hazy hills rise gently and recede behind our long bow wave. I dipped into a book, skipping paragraphs and pages the way I looked forward to skipping the problems and the tricky places that had dogged *Princess* all the way down the coast. This was the way to do the ditch.

She was a tidy little vessel. Eight feet of draft is too deep for comfort in the canal. It would be all right if she stayed in the channel. The pilothouse offered a fine view of the countryside. The cabins opening onto the main deck were quite pleasant, and the round galley table that conformed to the forward bulkhead gave the place a nice family atmosphere.

There was no family atmosphere at the table of the ST49 unless you count Ma Barker and her brood. The cook set the mood. His name was Napoleon. Napoleon was skinny, and hairless. His face folded at the mouth like Popeye. He wore a perpetual scowl. He could cook like an angel.

Roasted, stewed, fried, barbequed, baked, the chow was wildly wonderful. There were fancy pastries, dimpled dumplings, seductive salads, devastating desserts. But as soon as the Lucullian repast was spread before the crew Napoleon would go into his routine.

"Damn riffraff," he grumbled, "bums, you never had it so

2

good. Who thanks me for putting out a meal like this? Pearls before swine is what it is. When I think of the people that I have cooked for. Kings. Aristocracy. Statesmen. Captains of industry. I have cooked for the crown heads of Europe."

Old Captain Erbe, who knew what he was eating, turned in his chair and faced the cook. "I'll crown you." he said.

"The king of Belgium sent his minister to thank me."

"Keep talking and you'll need a minister."

"*Cochon,*" said Napoleon.

The fresh-water sailor said, "Look, Frog, who can stomach swill like this? Look at the meat. Raw."

"Barbarian," said Napoleon.

The mate muscled his way past the cook, knocking against the bulkhead with his shoulder. He drew a cup of coffee from the urn. "Sure now," he said to Napoleon, "it's a fine meal you cooked. Now why don't you shut up so we can enjoy it?"

"When does the music start?" said Immezzo Mari.

"Home was never like this," said the fresh-water sailor.

Mealtime on the ST49 was a three-ring circus. I got into the habit of loading up a plate and taking it up on the boat deck. There was always some corner of the fidley in the lee of the stack where the warmth of the engine, the passing view, and the quietude of acceptable sound made it as nice a place to eat as the Rainbow Room.

The rumble of the engine seemed to mute the rumble from the galley. Neither noise ever really popped off. It was strange. All that commotion and a total absence of gore. There was no blood spilled until the day the muscle-bound mate and the unintelligible engineer had a go at it on the dock in Norfolk.

Nobody knew what the fight was all about. Least of all the participants. Or even how the fight was arranged. There was a complete lack of communication. What the chief was saying, no one understood. What the mate had to say never made any sense.

We came into the harbor of Norfolk with a giant tanker on

our tail. The cook came up on the boat deck and demanded a word with the captain. That was the first inkling we had of the impending battle. The captain went back to talk to him.

"Captain," said Napoleon, "as a gambling man, I have five dollars that says the chief will whip the mate."

"Where's the fight?" said the captain.

"On the dock in Norfolk."

"You've got a bet." said the old man.

The mate, looking back from the pilothouse to where the captain was talking to the cook, suddenly saw his jacket, which he had carelessly hung on the handrail, picked up by a gust of wind and flung over the side. He grabbed the wheel from Immezzo Mari and put it hard over.

The old man bounced into the wheelhouse his eyes popping and swung the wheel back with all his weight. "What in the hell is the matter with you?"

The tanker swerved missing the ST49 by inches. "My jacket blew over the side."

"That's too damn bad."

"My wallet was in the pocket: All my papers."

"You came near getting us rammed." The old man glared at the mate wondering whether he hadn't put five dollars on the wrong horse.

Down in the engine room, the chief screamed at the oiler who gave up trying to understand and paid him no mind. There was little comfort past Old Point Comfort for either the chief or the wild-eyed mate.

The ST49 tied up at Lambert Point. The first one on the dock was the engineer. He stomped out on the concrete dock and waited with his hands clasped behind his back.

The mate came out of the cabin he shared with the old man, climbed down the ladder, and jumped out on the dock. They stood there in the winter sunshine with their fists up like in a woodcut of the old barrel-bellied fisticuff kings. Like two fourth-rate pugs, totally out of condition, hopelessly overweight and scared as hell of each other.

The pigeons strutting on the dock puffed and waddled around the two men's feet, circling them in the sun. Beyond the fat gladiators in a crystalline texture of sea and light lay the entrance to the busy harbor alive with the leisurely motion of ships pushing through brine. In the air, the planes slipping the restraint of earth were flying free and in formation.

The crowd on the tug and a couple of longshoremen waited in silence. The captain was on the boat deck leaning against the rail. The cook was hanging out of the galley doorway with a cigarette dangling from his lower lip. The rest of the crew had ringside seats from every vantage point of the vessel. Sitting on bits or leaning against a bulkhead, there was no sound, no gesture out of anyone. This was a family brawl.

The old man had told me about an awful fight on a dock in Melbourne. He looked over at me and winked. The fighters circled around each other for what seemed an eternity. Two fat men in their sweaty singlets and their baggy pants. At last the mate managed a right to the cheekbone of the chief. It drew a little blood. Then they circled, sparring like a couple of carnival bears that were sick and tired of standing up.

Wham! The engineer swung a roundhouse that landed on the mate's nose. It gave it a nice rosy glow. It also drew a drop of blood. The fight was over.

No one won. No one lost. As mysteriously as the fracas had started, it stopped. In the ancient tradition of the duel, honor had been achieved. The fighters left the dock and boarded the vessel. It was a lousy show.

"Wouldn't it be great if the war could be resolved as easy as that?" said Immezzo Mari the *basso profundo*.

It was time for lunch. The food was wonderful again. Napoleon, comforted by the dead heat, kept his big mouth shut. I ate in the galley. We shoved off down the Intracoastal Waterway at noon. I was at the wheel.

Everything was fine till we came to Money Point. Peterson was in the pilothouse. He had been hired for the voyage because of his intimate knowledge of the waterway. The chart was spread out on the chart table behind me. I looked around. Peterson was gone.

I made the turn to the left at Money Point the same way that I had with *Princess* under full sail. Then I blew for the bridge to open and rang the telegraph to stop the engine.

The bridge opened. I made the turn to the right and rang the telegraph again for half ahead. The captain, still munching on his lunch, came up the ladder to the wheelhouse. "Where's the second mate?" he said.

I shrugged. After we had passed the bridge the second mate came back. "Where in hell have you been?"

"I went down to get a cup of coffee."

"You went down to get a cup of coffee when we were coming on to a bridge?"

"Yah," said the "swamp admiral," jerking the wheel out of my hands. There is a four-foot spot on the left-hand side as you go between the towers. It is clearly marked on the chart. That's where Peterson put her aground.

The old man rang "Full Astern." Caught like a fat fish in a falling tide, the ST49, swinging her tail from port to starboard, struggled to free herself from the black ooze of industrial Norfolk. Great clouds of bottom went out to the left and the right as she thrashed. Slowly she inched herself back, and then suddenly she was free. The old man stopped the engine. As she drifted he turned to Peterson and said, "Go down and tell the cook that we'll be having dinner at eight o'clock."

As the "swamp admiral" walked out of the pilothouse, the captain said. "Peterson."

"Yes sir."

"Don't come back."

I took the wheel. I took the little vessel down through all the twists and turns to Great Bridge. Immezzo Mari spelled me through the Virginia Cut. I took her again through all the

6

crazy loops of North Landing River. We followed the buoys that stood like black sentinels down through the marshy river. There were ducks landing and taking off. The captain held her while I went for coffee. I sat on the cruciform bit forward sipping the hot stuff as we passed the spot where I had run *Princess* aground in a wild rush to get to Coinjock and register for the draft. Now I was back again in the ditch. We passed the schoolhouse in Coinjock where the draft board caught an inland sailor and chased him out to sea. It was hard to believe. It was also four o'clock. The mate came on watch.

I wasn't out of the wheelhouse ten minutes when the tough fresh-water sailor under the direction of the muscle-bound Irish mate put the tugboat hard and fast aground. He made the wrong turn at Number 23. Ran between two black markers and fetched up in the mud. The captain stormed out of his cabin and demanded to know what happened.

The mate, staring out of the wheelhouse window, said, "The red nun was in the sun."

This time the ST49 wouldn't come off. She roared and she shook in a frenzy of frustration. She slewed around and thrashed in bursts, but it wasn't any good. The engine couldn't budge her. We were going to have to kedge her off.

The massive lifeboat was pried from its chock, swung out on the davits, and lowered away. We wrestled the big kedge anchor over the side and lowered it into the boat. We rowed to the opposite bank dragging a two-inch cable. It took four of us.

There is a spoil area off Buck Landing Creek. We dropped the hook and Peterson took up the slack with the electric windlass aft. The anchor dragged across the channel.

We got the anchor up out of the mud and rowed it across again.

The tide began to come in. That helped. The anchor began to drag again as the windlass took up the slack. Then it snagged for a moment on a submerged log, giving the cable an extra yank. The propeller, chewing huge hunks of bottom, beat its way back out of the maw of muck. We were afloat.

It took the entire crew, engineers, cook, messmen, and deck gang to get the lifeboat back in its chocks on the boat deck. It was a major project. After that agony, the wheel was mine.

I did know the waterway. I had learned it the hard way. I had sailed all the way down, most of it under canvas a scant year before.

It was just like it was back on the *Princess*. I had the wheel to myself.

It is easier to con a vessel from a pilothouse that is better than twenty feet in the air. Easier than from the cockpit of a sailboat that is half under water. But the big advantage of the ST49 was the heavenly grub. Even if I did have to eat it off the fidley.

We ran the river till the first star came out. The old man staring out of the wheelhouse window at the darkening canal kept muttering, "The red nun was in the sun."

It became quiet. All you could hear was the throb of the diesel engine echoing across the countryside. The silence was broken by Napoleon, the cook:

"What's this jazz about dinner at eight?"

"You heard me," said Captain Erbe, "We are breaking watches and running during the hours of daylight."

"I'm cooking dinner at five," said Napoleon, "I don't give a damn if you eat it at midnight." The cook turned and climbed backward down the wheelhouse ladder.

"You know," said Captain Erbe. "I'd like to kick that Napoleon over the side."

He turned to me as I swung the wheel. "By the way," he said, "can you cook?"

It was funny. We laughed.

2

We dropped the hook in the lee of Camden Point as the night deepened. The ST49 crossed the Albemarle in the silence and the stillness of morning.

Squatting between her bow waves, the pudgy little tug ploughed through the hazy serenity of the Sound blithely unaware of its capacity for mayhem. She passed deep into the protection of the Alligator River before it too was aware that it had something to toy with. The tender overhatted little tug would have been no match for their most casual caprice.

I have watched the Albemarle shaping her sharp waves from the cockpit of *Princess*, and I have known the ferocity of her heavy water making up across sixty miles of shallow sea. We passed in among the trees and entered the long canal that cuts across the soggy country. We had watched the "drudgers" tonging oysters in the beds, and I knew damn well that Captain Erbe would be making an early port in some likely oyster settlement. Like "war is hell," and the oyster was in season.

I came back to the wheel at the headwater of the Pungo River and took her into Belhaven. I knew the way. We tied up alongside a shucking factory, and as unofficial representatives of the United States Army, we were invited to "hep" ourselves.

Some kids came aboard and wandered around the strange looking vessel that lay between a skipjack and a bugeye, both of which still carried the low freeboard, the long sprit, the sheer of deck, and the rake of spar that distinguished the American privateer. It was as if the ST49 had suddenly regressed into a half-forgotten era, which wouldn't have been a bad idea when you consider her chances of survival in the open sea.

We gorged ourselves. Like doomed men do. Or don't, according to their temperament. We did. All of us. There has never been in the township of Belhaven such a flagrant example of conspicuous consumption. Certainly not without horseradish sauce.

We took off at daylight with all the oysters we could carry. One of the Belhaven kids helping us undock ran his hand along the steel bulkhead of the little ship and said, "She is a hard boat."

How hard a boat she was remained to be seen. But no steel boat nor any synthetic vessel can ever match the sympathetic touch of wood. Watching the kids' eyes as they drifted over to where the beloved skipjack lay, I had an awful hunger for *Princess,* my little wooden Friendship sloop. And all the wooden boats of long ago.

We had fried oysters for breakfast and oyster bisque at tiffin time. The air of the north was clear and cold, and sometimes before the sun came up over the flat land that separated us from the sea, there would be a tinge of frost on the edge of the marsh grass.

This was painters' country. The wind-combed parallels of reed rose out of their own reflection at high water, the flow of light into grey-green and earth-umber was managed without pose or pretense. The sky shared its abstract prism with the folded impression of the land. They say that when the guns speak, the muse is silent. The war years are bad years for the painter. Or for anyone in the peaceful arts that cannot be readily geared to the wheels of war.

Immezzo Mari played the fiddle. He sang. You couldn't hear him for the strident sounds of conflict. I paint. Nature said, "Look but don't touch." I looked.

Harry, the oiler, had a talent so transcendent that one might honestly say that here was one of the most unique performers in the world, war or peace. Harry talked to dogs.

No one on the vessel knew about Harry's ability. Not until Harry got a load in Belhaven and woke the whole town by calling on all the dogs to join him in a triumphant evocation. At two o'clock in the morning.

The entire town was roused out. The constable came out too, but there wasn't a damn thing he could do about it. Nobody could put the finger on Harry. The dogs clammed up.

Where Harry picked up this special talent was something we could never find out. He could unquestionably get on the canine wave length and play it for all it was worth. George, the lanky first assistant, told us about it.

It wasn't until we had passed all the way down to Beaufort and tied up in Morehead City that I got a chance to sample Harry's astounding virtuosity.

It was a wonderful run. We came out of the Pungo River with the wind on our starboard quarter, and we passed a loaded skipjack beating into Belhaven. Crossing the Pamlico River we elected to duck behind Goose Creek Island. The tough talking A.B. spelled me at the canal and the Hobucken Swing Bridge deferred to the war grey of the ST49 by swinging wide long before we had occasion to sound the triple-blasted theme.

I held her through the travail of a following northeaster that swept down the length of the Pamlico, up the Neuse River, and into the quiet embrace of Adam's Creek. At the end of the long canal we came quickly into port. God help us had we tried to make it from Norfolk outside. As we tied up, the old man glanced out at the booming surf that sloshed in across Frying Pan Shoals. His eyes turned for a look at the top-heavy little trap that we were soon to take out into the kind of water that he knew. I thought I saw him shake his head. Then he went down the ladder to have dinner.

There was an elaborate smörgasbord all set up. Napoleon said, "Help yourselves," and shoved off. I grabbed a bite, got dressed, and went ashore with Immezzo Mari and Harry the oiler. Morehead City is my town.

There were a lot of Richards (very early) hanging in Morehead City. When I went by in *Princess* I had painted up a storm. Every fisherman had one. A picture of his vessel, a sketch of his kid, an impression of a pogy boat or of a new one on the ways in the process of construction. The fellow who owned the fish wharf had taken one in exchange for a dozen meals. It hung right above the cash register. They were all painted on a new kind of watercolor paper that had the habit of eating up the paint. There was too much sulphite or something in the paper.

I took Harry and Immezzo Mari around to see my paintings, or what was left of them. Some of them had improved in the process of disintegration, like the Samothrace had or the Parthenon. All in a year's time, which is progress of a kind. We ended up in a gin mill.

We drank Four Roses. One at a time. We drank in silence. The three of us were all thinking the same thing. No one spoke. The question pervaded the place like a wild scrawl in soap on the mirror over the bar. It didn't say "Merry Christmas" or even "Happy Halloween." It said to us with a flourish of a question mark and a lacey filigree of suds, *"Can The ST49 Sail The Ocean Blue?"*

I tried to tell Harry the oiler about the menhaden fishing vessel that my friend Asa used to build in Morehead City with nothing more than a circle on the floor of his shop for a plan.

"I don't believe it," said Harry.

"How big was it?" said Immezzo Mari.

"Two hundred and fifty feet."

"You're dreaming," said Harry.

"Come on, I'll show you."

"Where are the girls?" said Immezzo Mari

We went to Asa's yard. I showed Harry the mark on the floor. Asa was sitting on a planer whittling a toothpick. There was no vessel being built.

"Asa, how come you're not building vessels for the government?"

"We can't read their damn plans," said Asa.

"Where are the girls?" said Immezzo Mari.

We went looking for the girls. There was a kind of USO party at the big house on the corner. As Merchant Marine boys, we were given a wary welcome. A seaport town is always leery of a sailor.

The girls were sympathetic, polite, distant. Immezzo Mari got acquainted with a cute little brunette. We listened to local chitchat, and we heard a broadcast about the four freedoms that we were fighting for. The punch they served us contributed little enough to our quest for the fifth freedom, the freedom that came in fifths. Freedom from pain. Harry and I landed in another bar.

I ran into old Jake Frankly, of Morehead City, to whom everybody was a spy until he proved himself innocent. If you could hold your liquor you were innocent. We were innocent.

We drifted back in the general direction of the tug, dragging old Jake with us, and we ran into Immezzo Mari who was in one hell of a hurry. It seemed that the cute little brunette had a boyfriend, and the boyfriend was home unexpectedly on leave.

"Come on. Let's go," said Immezzo Mari.

"Let's have another drink," said Jake Frankly.

"Don't you understand? He's after me," said Immezzo.

"I'll fix him," said Harry the oiler. That's when Harry opened up with his call to the dogs.

It didn't sound like much of a call. It wasn't a bark and it wasn't a yip. It couldn't be called a yelp and it wasn't a snarl, but whatever it was, it set up a squall that you could hear for miles. Every dog in Morehead City came alive with a holler and a bellow and a fit of frenzied barking. It was unbelievable. It got Immezzo Mari off the hook and the whole town out into the streets. The dogs were still howling when we got back to the ST49.

It was damn near dawn. We had coffee in the galley of the ST49. We felt very little pain, but Jake Frankly was stoned. He said, "This is a damn Yankee gunboat and you're all a bunch of spies."

We laid him out gently on the wharf, and we shoved off down the Intracoastal Waterway as the soft light of day came up across the fury of Hatteras.

We passed into the long crooked rivers linked by the tedious canals. The weary waterway, the unmitigated sameness of cypress swamp, the aimless backwater bog, and the dead-end bayou were beginning to pale on the old man. You could see it in the pained expression on his face.

Captain Erbe, after forty-five years at sea, could take only so much of the ditch. As it led us down toward Charleston he began to take a wildly possessive interest in the fragmentary glimpses of the open sea.

We saw the blue water beyond the forbidding shoals of Bogue Inlet. We caught another glimpse of it across the pale green reeds that choke New River Inlet, and we caught intermittent flashes of it all the way down to Wrightsville Beach.

Yet, for all the sameness and the monotony of the Intracoastal Waterway, the ocean seemed to offer a repetitious quality that was extravagantly preferable to the endless untenanted stretches of the land. Whether the ST49 could live in deep water became an academic question. We became absorbed in the interminable windings and turnings of this primeval intestinal tract. We ran the ranges of Cape Fear River with the sun in our eyes and tied up at Southport for the night.

We were off again at sun-up, and the other deck hands spelled me down through the uncomplicated canals. We stopped for a moment in McClellanville, which is my favorite Confederate town, and we came into Charleston by starlight. The town was as beautiful as ever. More so by night. The temptation to run out of the Copper, Wondo, and Ashley rivers and out to sea was nobly resisted, and we were off again at dawn into the boggy bush.

Every passing hour another name. James, Johns, Wadmalaw, Dawho, Edisto, Jehossee, Samson, Coosaw, and the town of Beaufort for lunch. The proud old brick buildings presented to the river the same facade as they did during the Civil War.

We passed between Parris Island, which was alive with purpose, and Saint Helena, which was dead as death. We lowered the hook alongside Skidaway for the night and swung with the tide, like some prehistoric steel monster in an antediluvian morass, with the anachronistic man on watch snoring his fool head off.

Another long day up and down the rivers, now with the tide and then against it, Ogeechee, Ossabaw, Saint Catherine, Debby, Altamaha, Buttermilk, Saint Simon, Saint Andrews, Saint Mary's River and suddenly Fernandina.

Our orders said to go all the way to Jacksonville inside, but

Captain Erbe had a way of interpolating orders. He was also forty years over draft age, so there was damn little the Army could do about it. We went outside.

We took on water, galley supplies, and a landing barge in tow, and off we went into the great unknown.

As the tiny top-heavy harbor tug with her burden bucked through the roaring surf, old Captain Erbe began to look younger every minute. It seemed as if the marks of care and strain that come with the years were brushed from his face by the southeasterly and the aspect of open sea.

We passed the last breaking surf wave, and the ST49 struck bravely out to gain the ease of deep water and the long swing of ocean. She did all right.

The wind was what the captain called a "gentle breeze." Actually it was half a gale. We swung with the wave action like a pendulum. As the wind stiffened we rolled even more.

It was not too bad during the hours of daylight, but as night came on and the sea grew in violence with the mounting storm, a curious kind of satisfaction began to show on the old man's face. Short of capsizing, the ST49 was doing exactly what a deep-sea man might expect of her. The acid test came late that night off Canaveral. We damn near went over.

I was scared to death. The old man loved it.

3

It was the sixth day of February in the year 1943. A little boy pulling a toy boat along the sandy bank of the St. Mary's River watched as a 65-foot harbor tug with an Army landing barge in tow headed out to sea from the Port of Fernandina.

The tide came in quickly with the wind and the toy boat toppled in the whipping hemline of surf. The tug and its barge became tiny specks that were lost to the eye and found, lost and found in the heavy respiration of the sea.

The tug was the *ST49*. She was owned by the Army, and she was manned by a civilian crew. Of the ten men who made up her complement, there was every conceivable kind of kook. A guy had to be plain nutty, or nutty about boats to be on board.

The *ST49* was top heavy, overhatted as any toy boat you can buy loaded with gismos. She was something for a kid to pull with a string along the beach. Her big hat was the steel pilothouse. Add a solid steel mast, a steel deck house and fidley, and an enormous ornamental steel stack and you have the *ST49*, endlessly in search of her center of gravity.

So was her crew. The sea couldn't care less.

The wind from the southeast gathered weight. Before you

could turn around, it was blowing a full gale. It blew without pity, without meaning, it blew for the hell of it. A summary hell for the sins of war.

Manned by ten Americans who were innocently engaged in the "effort," the little tug stood up to it like the spirit of redemption, teetering, all-forgiving, hopeful. She piled into the ever-mounting torrent that exploded beneath her meager forefoot with a compulsive curiosity. A welter of foam curled along her house like a boa constrictor with the itch. The wind leaned against her topsides in overwhelming spasms of affection mouthing a groan that seemed to say, "For God's sake, go back."

The old man, Captain Erbe, and the tug spoke another language. In their vocabulary the word for retreat was scratched. There was no synonym for surrender. It would have been hopeless anyhow. To turn and try to make port again in the violent caprice of that sea would have been to court the disastrous certainty of a broach. Captain Louis Erbe hugged the frame between the pilothouse windows and stared ahead into the deepening gloom of nightfall.

I was at the wheel. As we drew away from the compounded misery of beach and current, the rollers leveled off into the long hills and the easy valleys of good water. Now the quartering action of the *ST49* began to pay off in the regular dividends of deep sea. We had made our easting, and nothing more terrible lay ahead than the Gulf Stream and the cursed Canaveral at night. The old man turned against the edge of gloam, cleared his throat, and said, "So you're an artist."

"Yes," I said.

"I'll tell you a story," said Captain Erbe. The wind moaned and the sea salivated against the side. The freeing ports banged shut in protest and were overwhelmed across the low bulwarks of the little ship. I put the wheel down bringing her up to quarter another wave and waited.

"I was on the beach in Frisco," he said. "I went into this

bar and ordered a drink. Looking up I noticed a calendar on the bulkhead behind the bar. It had a painting of a square-rigged ship on it. The bartender poured me a shot of rye. I kept looking at that picture of a ship."

As the sun slid beneath the horizon there was a hint of fair weather in the fiery fringe of the leaden sky. The old man spoke again. "There was something about that ship. The reverse curve of her bow, the fineness of her entrance, the sheer of her deck. She was also a main skys'l yarder. It had to be the *Abner Coburn.* I ordered another drink. While the barkeep was pouring it, I pulled a dollar out of my wallet and my certificate of discharge off the *Abner Coburn* and spread it out on the bar."

The tug buried her nose in a snarling comber that sloshed clear up to the pilothouse, tossing a rag of spray across the wheel. I ducked and wiped my eyes with the sleeve of my jacket. The old man turned and grinned. "When the barkeep picked up my dollar he saw the discharge paper of the *Abner Coburn* on the bar. 'What's this?' he says."

The old man hung on as the little tug rocked in the boiling sea. "Take the paper and read the name of the ship on the calendar," We quartered another giant comber. "*Abner Coburn*" he read, "*Abner Coburn,* 1896, holy smokes." We passed into more reasonable water. The old man man was silent. Then he said, "I've still got that paper in my wallet."

It was quite dark now and the *ST49* settled down to an easy quartering action as the course was changed to south by east. "I had to have one of those calendars. The barkeeper sent me down to the office of the Columbian Rope Company. 'Look at this,' I said, showing my discharge certificate. They gave me a calendar," The old man stopped talking for a while. Then he said, "I've still got that calendar at home."

There didn't seem to be any more to say. The old man had the calendar, and the end of the war was nowhere in sight. The little tug hammered away at the persistent sea, and nothing was settled. "So you are an artist," said the old man.

"Yes," I said again.

"Suppose you could make me a copy of that painting in oil?"

I was on the spot. "Captain," I said, "I'd like to do that for you. You must realize that an artist who copies other paintings is known as a hack. There used to be a lot of them. They were called museum lice. Printing did away with all that," The old man meditated on the idea nodding his head.

"Yeah, yeah," he said. There was no other objection except perhaps the rumble of the diesel or the "sheesh" of the sea.

"No artist worth his salt would copy the work of another painter," I had the old man in a corner.

There was a long silence. "How about that," he said, "seeing that picture of the *Abner Coburn* on the barroom bulkhead?"

"It sure was something."

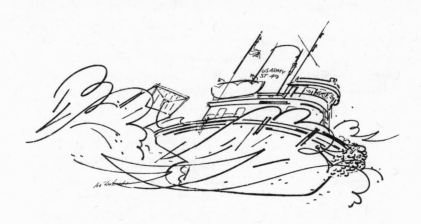

The mate came on watch. It was midnight and the fresh-water sailor took my place at the wheel. The old man stayed in the pilothouse. I went below and tried to get some sleep. I dreamed about painted ships on painted oceans coming to life in giant seas of cataclysmic reality. It was no dream. The little tug was swinging to the bitter edge of her ability to right herself. I put on a life jacket and went on deck.

Mezzo Mari was on the boat deck. "Do you think she'll go over?" he said.

"You better get a life jacket."

"Mine is in the wheelhouse."

"I'll get it for you." I edged along the gyrating boat deck hanging on to the handrail until I got around to where the old man was leaning out of the pilothouse window. "Captain," I said, "would you hand me the life jacket that's under the chart table?"

He reached down and handed it to me. There was a smile bisecting his full face. "You afraid she'll go over?" I took the jacket.

I felt like a damn fool with two jackets. I gave one to Immezzo Mari. By the time we got around Cape Canaveral I wished I had four jackets. Why that vessel didn't go over in the turbulence of the cape, I will never know. Plenty of them did. The sheer anxiety of it brought on such fatigue that I finally hit the sack, jacket and all, and fell into the kind of sleep that only a wildly swinging cradle can induce.

The wind moderated with the morning. We swung down close along the shore to beat the stream and we sighted an Army tug identical to ours and with an identical landing barge in tow. They were headed north. We hailed them. "Where you headed?"

The answer was the story of World War II. The story of all wars. "New York," they yelled. We looked at each other. That was our port of departure. We resumed our course and left the other tug wagging in the wind, as we did, like two clowns in the hopeless and desperate employment of a congenital idiot. The mission of the *ST49* was patently as far out as her center of gravity.

I went on watch again at eight, and we passed, one after another, the great lights that guard the Keys from the yawing errors of little boats and the tragic misdirection of great keels. It had begun to blow again, and the warm and gentle easterly that drifted across the Bahamian banks grew into a violent duster that heaped the seas across the quarter and leaned in pounding pulsations against the house.

The captain checked the chart and adjusted the course to favor deep water and sea room. Then he said, "Wasn't that something, seeing that painting of the *Abner Coburn* in the bar?"

I allowed that it was. But the old man was like a bulldog with a bone. "If I can't get the original oil painting of that ship, do you suppose you can paint me a copy of the calendar?"

I went into my spiel about artistic integrity. I sounded off, this time in depth, pointing out that even painting from nature was becoming unacceptable. Painters of importance were busy creating forms of their own, many of which had only the vaguest connection with reality. As far as the *Abner Coburn* was concerned, forget it. The old man swallowed hard.

"It sure was something, seeing that picture of her on the bulkhead of that barroom." He stared into the night wrapped in some far-off reverie of square-rigged ships and spicy ports down under, while the wind leaped in an inexplicable fury.

We were now down off The Elbow with a good chance of making Key West by the early hours of morning. As we edged around past Molasses Key, Alligator Key, and Sombrero, the wind slid around to our quarter. At last, as we approached Sand Key, the wind was dead astern, and the following sea was climbing on our backs.

The force of the gale was such that the barge came charging along behind us as if it were under power. As we passed American Shoal, and edged close to turn north, the seas that bucked the force of the Gulf Stream were of such violence, of such steepness and magnitude, that it seemed like absolute suicide to attempt a right-angle turn into Key West.

Here was the moment of truth they talk about. The confrontation of man and the eternal force of nature. In that moment the strength of your own arms, the judgment of your own eye, and all the force of your own being must prevail. Here the biggest, the strongest, the most skillful must take charge. The biggest and the strongest was the burly Irishman watching wide-eyed. Suddenly he grabbed the wheel away from me and made the turn.

All hell broke loose. The *ST49* rolled down into a sea and scooped a great draught of green water into her pilothouse, She was a goner. I hung on.

The old man gripped the window frame as the sea came plunging through. The Irishman fell to the deck blubbering and screaming. I grabbed the wheel and spun her up into the wind. In that moment, given the momentum of thrust, the huge propeller righted the vessel and the waist-high sea slid out through the pilothouse door.

"Hard right," the old man yelled. The massive wall of water moved in again for the kill.

"I've got her hard right."

"Take it off."

"Midships," I said.

"Here it comes again. Hard over."

"Hard right," I said. "I've got her, Captain."

This time she quartered the huge sea. She did it the next time and the time after that and every time. I spun the wheel into every giant comber that came charging at us like the ultimate bull, dripping gore and breathing death. Now the sea came flying through the open pilothouse windows in sheets of spray, and the Irish mate, whose brain had been rocked by some recent torpedo blast, lay shuddering and moaning in the slosh, lost in the incoherent and multiple recollection of crises.

It seemed like forever before the final wild wave threw its savage weight against our vulnerable topsides. At last the very reef, whose voracious jaws had ripped the bottom out of countless unsuspecting vessels, screened the onslaught with its angry teeth and fed us only the endless train of trammeled wavelets. We were safe. We were in. I hit the sack, soaking wet, and slept.

The barge was delivered to the Navy base. The voyage had scarcely begun but we had won the first round.

I slept until noon. As soon as I could struggle to my feet I drifted into town and found an artist's supply shop. With a new canvas and my little set of oil paints, I sat under a banyan tree and reconstructed the scene as it might have looked to the eye of a fish at Sand Key. The *ST49* laying way over, the sea cascading through her ports and over her house. The scudding grey clouds and the violent opalescent green sea in league with that crazy barge doing their best to turn us over. You live it all again that way.

I was proud of the painting. I bought a suitable frame and brought it back to the ST49. I handed the painting to the old man. "Here you are Captain Erbe, this is for you."

He took the painting in his hands. Then he took one hand and fetched his glasses out and put them on. Maybe because there was an honest-to-God tear in his eye.

It was something.

4

Old Captain Erbe was hooked on ships. He was obsessed with the tall squarerigged ships of his youth. He loved the fast steel ships that crowded the squareriggers into oblivion. He couldn't kick the habit even when it came to the irascible harbor tug that he was taking to San Francisco.

You could see it in the way he fussed over the *ST49*. The lines had to be faked down, the decks scrubbed, the pilot-house painted. It was a love that was transferred from one vessel to the next with the easy grace of a practiced Don Juan. The older he got and the rounder, the more love he came to have for the homely little boat that he commanded.

The enthusiasm that all seamen have for a vessel of any description became in Erbe a kind of double standard. He shared that affection with an abiding love for the bride he had taken in his declining years.

"Joe," he would say in the semidarkness of the pilothouse while he stared ahead in his beady-eyed search for the menace to navigation that had his number on it. "Joe," he'd say with a fierce inflection as he turned and stared at me momentarily to give the declaration its full impact, "I love my wife."

It was a nice thing to hear from an old man who had his

25

ninth issue of his master's license for sail and steam. He said it with the same tone of voice he used to order the hook dropped, the springline eased, or the course changed.

He didn't talk too much about the vessels he had known over the years, the endless procession of ships that had shared his salty libido. But he did talk about horses.

Captain Erbe would put his last buck on the nose of a nag. What he wouldn't risk at sea in the wild gamble of life and death, he threw with a plunging recklessness to the bookies. He didn't give a damn about the vicissitudes, the hardship, the deprivation of old age. He gambled for the hell of it. He took the kick of winning and the blow of losing to sea with him in a rollicking feel for the goddess of chance. Pressed into service as a bookmark in his Bowditch was the latest tip sheet, which he studied with the concentration of a Rhodes scholar.

Coming into port, when any other skipper might be concerned with the vagaries of shoal and shore, depth and direction, Captain Erbe would turn to me and bark, "Joe, by your reckoning, how many furlongs would you say it is to that sea buoy?" Then he would laugh. So would I. The race track was home port.

There were no race tracks in Key West. There were plenty of spit and polish Navy sailors and military police who busied themselves rounding up our crew. They claimed we were out of uniform. They were right. We were.

It was hot. Some of our crew who had been trained at St. Petersburg wore the white cap and the bell-bottom pants. To hell with the middy blouse. It was too damn girlish.

When old Captain Erbe came stomping down the main drag dressed in khaki pants and a singlet with the omelet of a master on the visor of his cap, the Navy threw in the sponge.

Whether the Navy approved or not, whatever he wore was clean. The captain did his own laundry. He'd be out on the boat deck in fair weather with a couple of buckets, his hairy arms immersed in suds, a cigar in his mouth and his gold bespangled cap set at a jaunty angle on his head. The money he saved doing his own wash did little to recoup the losses he sustained at the track, but it made him feel better about it.

The week's wash was hung on a manila line that was strung along the boat deck. Each garment was secured by tucking the ends between the strands of the line. There were no clothespins on the *ST49*.

Erbe was a civilian sailor. He was trained in the long harsh school of mercantile shipping, where rewards are equated to performance, and the reward for seniority is a berth in Sailor's Snug Harbor or a sympathy job as crum boss. The Navy begged him to accept a reserve commission. He turned it down, and they respected him because he was good.

When the Navy orders were handed to him with specific instructions as to the course he must follow in the run to New Orleans, he winked at me, shoved the orders in the chart table drawer and proceeded to follow a course imposed by the higher authority of wind, weather, and the mercurial nature of the sea. We got there.

Most didn't. It was not until the end of the war that I found out how many of these tugs had been lost by capsizing. It was like being told that you had sleepwalked across Niagara Falls on a tightrope.

For the time being we elected to ignore much of the terror inherent in the operation, and we went along with Captain Erbe who obviously knew how to live. We fished. The captain fashioned a fishing line by winding some white toweling into a fish shape on a stout wire leader. The homemade lure dangled a heavy hook and the quarter-inch swiveled line was fastened to the railing on the boat deck. We left Key West at noon.

There was a heavy snatch block secured as a weight on the line just above the after platform. When the fish struck, the weight of the snatch block took the shock, banging away on the deck in a commotion that would wake the dead. It got to be a nuisance. Bonito after bonito were hauled aboard, unhooked, and flung back into the lovely blue stream. It became so frequent that we were about to take in the line when the dolphin struck.

, It was a big beauty. It took the hook like a tiger, announcing its disappointment and wrath in violent hammer blows of the snatch block as the line thrashed. There is no visual experience to match the sight of a dolphin in its death throes. The flaming evanescence of luminous lemon bleeding into emerald, punctuated by spots of shining royal blue, is without its counterpart in the kingdom of living things. The color faded fast like fogged film. In the hands of Napoleon the cook, it came to life again briefly in the poetry of Spanish sauce. It was good eating.

Erbe was a fisherman. His technique was borrowed from sailing ship practice where there is no patience for the momentary luff to boat a fish. He caught them on the run.

We made good time. We ran north after rounding Tortugas along the west coast of Florida. The wind shifted from the prevailing southeasterly to the north. We took it broad on the starboard bow across the Gulf of Mexico. It was a pleasant run. Napoleon, figuring that he had a genuine gourmet in the old man, outdid himself. His cooking was a delight and a disservice. He spoiled us.

The sea became brown. We picked up the pilot at the sea buoy off the delta of the Mississippi and we made the hundred-mile run to New Orleans against the rush of the land-laden water. The impact of the river, the enormous gush of fresh water carrying with it the wealth of valleys and the one-way tide of a national watershed, was lost on no one. Most of the crew were farm boys, and they watched wide-eyed as the panorama spread. They saw lowland overwhelmed and new land tumbled up in a swelling valley of stolen soil through which the river continued night and day to carry its furtive burden. We saw giant trees sag under the overweening gift of fresh water and the good earth in solution. Here, where

America is bleeding, where the arterial flow takes its toll of the fertile soil and feeds it in sickening profusion to the fishes, life is lived at its exuberant best.

In New Orleans, neither war nor rationing nor the spiraling cost could abate the pace of high living nor stem the abundance of good food. Prepared by the master chefs of the fabulous restaurants, it provided a challenge to our cook Napoleon that he met head on. In this ultimate test of his skill and virtuosity he came up with the most sumptuous spreads that ever graced a banquet table. God help you if you weren't on board at four bells to eat it.

Captain Erbe, on his way back from the Navy office, drifted past the doors of Antoine's. He was seduced by the aroma that came out with the happy smiling diners. In he went. It was a fatal error.

As he sauntered back to the tug at about nine with a toothpick in his mouth, he was confronted by Napoleon. The hairless little cook, looking like an outraged housewife, stood waiting for him perched on the bulwark outside the galley door.

Before Napoleon could let go the blast, Captain Erbe beat him to the punch. "Napoleon," he said, "I'm sick and tired of your lip. You're fired."

Napoleon was crushed. He turned in stunned silence and walked away. He came back stinking drunk about an hour later and proceeded to shuffle around the main deck of the *ST49* spewing forth his entire repertory of profanity in an assumptive bass that made him a living prototype of Donald Duck. As he padded about, old Captain Erbe stretched out in his bunk with a belly full of good food and growled, "You had it coming to you," and flaked out.

In the estimation of Peterson, the swamp admiral, Napoleon was crazy lucky. Peterson wanted out. In his opinion it was only a matter of time before the little *ST49* would roll over and go down. He didn't want to be around when that happened. He badgered the old man constantly to let him pay off. Useless as he was, the old man took a fiendish delight in denying the second mate that fond desire.

The next morning in a wild confrontation Peterson approached the old man, his eyes bulging and his jaw quivering.

"Captain," he said, "you've got to pay me off."

"Why have I got to?"

"Because," said Peterson, who shared the master's quarters, "I've got syphilis and you'll probably catch it."

What he had was a weak stomach wall. Lucky for him it was all he needed to separate him from the *ST49*. He was all hearts and flowers when he left for the Marine Hospital for the lesser jeopardy of the surgeon's knife.

The old man made no fuss when the crazy mate paid off. He shrugged and said, "Joe, did you ever hear about rats deserting a ship?"

"I've heard about it. They say the ship is doomed."

"It happened one time in Melbourne. The rats came up out of the hold one after another and scampered ashore. They crawled out along the hawsers and dove off the bulwark to the dock. Half the crew got windy and went with them. The captain was an old squarehead by the name of Swanson. Toughest man I ever met. He said, 'Good riddance.' We shipped with a new crew. Bound for Boston around the Horn."

"Did you make it?"

"Hell yes. Best passage I ever made. The Straights of Magellan were like Chesapeake Bay. What in hell do rats know about ships?"

When Peterson paid off, I had hopes of getting his job. From his point of view, the old man had a better idea. He wanted to keep me on the wheel. The only alternative was to get a job as mate on another vessel. There were plenty of jobs as mate open in New Orleans, but the climate for such a maneuver had become increasingly unfavorable. But you never know.

The old man was an ambitious young fellow way back. Maybe he would recommend me. It became a question of asking at the proper moment. We took off one afternoon and swung into town in the trolley that was called Desire.

We walked down Royal Street. We passed along the black wrought-iron lace of portico and garden gate. We wandered along the cobbled sreets of the French Quarter, stopping at a telegraph office where Erbe wired some money home to his wife. We wound up in a gin mill.

A bookmaker was handling race track bets through a window as wide open as the ticket office down at the L & M. The names of the horses were posted. We sat at a table and ordered schooners of beer for a quarter that used to cost a nickel. There was a horse in the fourth race called Fleetheels.

I liked the name. I liked the idea of a horse called Fleetheels. I liked the beer. "Captain," If you have to bet, bet on Fleetheels. I have a powerful hunch that he will win."

"Yeah, yeah," said Erbe, and off he went to the window with a sawbuck in his big hand. Fleetheels was a ten-to-one shot.

He waited. The race was run. Somewhere out in Pimlico, Yonkers, or Hialeah. The important thing was that Fleetheels won. I congratulated the old man. He smiled. "Have another beer," he said.

We drank to victory. "Aren't you going to get your money?"

"Yeah, yeah," said Captain Erbe. "Have another beer." We drank up.

"How about your winnings?" I reminded the captain.

"Let me tell you something," said the old man.

"What's that?"

"On the way to the window I changed my mind."

"No."

"Yeah."

I sat there trying to figure the old man, wondering whether I would have had the same luck if I were a gambling man.

"Captain." I said, "they tell me that there are a lot of jobs as mate here in New Orleans for men with experience. A fellow don't need a license. I need a recommendation."

Captain Erbe looked at me. I knew what he was thinking. Here was I, the latest rat, all set to jump ship. I smiled. It was up to him. He knew that I'd be glad to stay with the *ST49* as top heavy as she was, if he were willing to promote me to mate. But then I wouldn't be at the wheel where he wanted me. We had another beer and got up to go. I steered him over to the crewing office at the Port of Embarkation.

Captain Louis Erbe got the red carpet when he came in. They hadn't seen a master of sail and steam in the place since it was established. He sat across from Higgins, the crewing director, and puffed a cigar.

"Well, Captain," said Higgins. "what about this fellow Richards?"

Two words were all the captain had to offer in my behalf. That's all it took. Two words, and I was mate on the *T45* bound for Panama.

Those two words were all the recommendation that anybody needs. I worked for them. The two words were, "He's willing."

That's all it took, but he said it again to make sure.

5

My separation from the *ST49* was managed with a minimum of misgiving. I grabbed my sea bag and blew.

That voyage from New York to New Orleans was one of the most hectic passages I can remember. The tender quality of that top-heavy trap had everybody on edge. What might have been an average voyage plagued with the usual smattering of ineptitude became, on that tug, an unending waltz with oblivion.

I was happy to stow my gear aboard the *T45*, which was tied up at the end of the long wharf at the Port of Embarkation. You would have been happy, too. She was a honey.

Of all the bottoms, great and small, which go to make up the vast Army Transport Fleet, there is none so endearing to the small boat dreamer as the T-boat. One look at her and the war faded, the sun rose through the interlacing shimmer of palm fronds out of a tranquil sea across the lagoon, and a little interisland freighter lowered her hook as the native boats clustered around her in happy salutation. She had everything.

Her sixty feet were just enough to bridge the average angry sea. She had beam and style. The flare of her bow, the sheer of her deck, and the easy run aft to the sweet curve of her transom pronounced her handy, sea-kindly, and able.

She had a two-hundred-and-fifty-horse diesel in her engine room and headroom to work it. She was provided with a good size deckhouse aft that held a head and accommodation for ten bunks. Her pilothouse amidship had a settee that was suitable for the master's bunk. A cargo hold forward, of enormous capacity, had a mast before it, fitted with a stout derrick boom. The strange thing about the vessel, classed as a cargo-personnel carrier, was the placement of the galley. It was jammed in the forepeak complete with coal stove, sink, galley table, a bunk for the cook, and nothing but a little mushroom ventilator for air. The refrigerator was aft in the deckhouse, which was insane.

One look at that galley and no cook worth his salt would sign on. We got a raw-boned kid from Texas who turned out to be a wild mixture of Godsend and disaster. His name was Bill. If he had a last name, no one knew it. He'd bite your head off if you talked to him.

The captain had not showed up when I went aboard. I had a cup of coffee with Bill and took a better look around. She was fully found. That's what they said, but I'd be damned if I could find the stuff. Stores, gear, and supplies were dumped into the hold like a cargo of coal. Breakfast cereal, tins of food, drums of oil, spare line and anchor, engine parts, and bed sheets were scrambled around as though in a blender. It was definitive chaos. I went to work.

I lashed the drums of oil to a stanchion. I dragged some dunnage down and boxed off the food stores. I roped down the engine parts to keep them from battering through the ceiling and out the sides. I wrestled alone in that hold as Jacob wrestled with the angel, sweating in the heat of New Orleans and gasping for breath in the dusty hold. The old man showed up at four o'clock.

The "old man" was twenty-one. He had pink cheeks and a blue suit. He had a gold stripe on his sleeve and the gall of a brass monkey. He was no sailor. This was the article known as a "ninety-day wonder." He introduced himself as "Captain Lawrence." Commendably resisting the temptation to help, he took off immediately to attend to some paper work and/or some broad registered at the Monteleone.

I had just about finished the job of getting the *T45* ready for sea when I was transferred to a sister ship, the *T44*. She was in the same sorry shape. There was nobody aboard.

I went to work hauling, sorting, roping, and wrestling. By the end of the day I was dragging. The vessel was almost squared away when the new captain came aboard to take over his command. He was a scared, diffident kid. I felt sorry for him then. I still do.

The next morning they called me to the crewing office. Higgins, the crewing director, was sitting at his desk. I came in panting and covered with dust. "Joe," he said, "I am putting you back aboard the *T45*. Take her down the river for fuel oil. I'll put someone on board who knows the way."

I looked at the man. This business of being executive officer was getting to be very unfunny. I shrugged and went to get my sea bag. Back on the *T45* I found that she now had a chief engineer named Murphy and a bespectacled kid called Jones to help him. The country boy from Texas was sweating it out as cook. "Captain" Lawrence was still in town on "ship's business." The man who knew the way was waiting for me in the pilothouse. He was a dark-complected character with a shifty look. I figured him for a descendant of the Arcadian Frenchmen who settled in the Louisiana bayous during the seventeenth century—or more likely an offspring of the cut-throats whose only allegiance was to the pirate Lafitte. When he spoke I could almost see the bandanna on his head, the patch on one eye, and the cutlass in his teeth.

We shoved off downstream pulling in to a long dock on the opposite bank, ten miles below New Orleans. It was late in the day before our turn came and our bunkers were filled.

Coming back, we had a dozen of the men who worked on the oil dock as passengers. The 'Cadian pilot suggested that we run close along the bank to avoid the heavy current. It was a good idea. I brought her in as close as I dared.

The 'Cadian wasn't happy. He demanded that we go even closer. There was no chart of the river on board. There were rocks visible along the bank. This was my first trip as officer. I had a lot to lose.

The Frenchman seethed. I paid him no mind and held my course. It was a short run. We tied up. I checked the lines. The passengers and the pilot filed off the boat. Standing on the dock I turned for another look at the bow line. Someone had kicked it loose.

The vessel began to swing in the heavy back eddy toward a high wharf that was bound to sheer the superstructure clean off. I jumped aboard, grabbed the bow line and leaped from the after deck to the dock with the bitter end of it in my hand. I snubbed the line and made it fast to the nearest bitt. I had an enemy. A nice, clean-cut, patriotic enemy who would sacrifice a hundred thousand dollars' worth of government property to fix my fanny. It took me two hours to horse that vessel back alongside the dock against the raging current. Then I went looking for him. We were both lucky. I never found him. The captain came aboard with all the charts from New Orleans to Panama and two deck hands, and we shoved off.

We ran the Intracoastal Waterway all the way to Panama City. We headed out to cross the northeast corner of the Gulf of Mexico when the captain fell victim to a sickness associated with the sea. I stowed him aft for future reference and took command of the vessel. Now and again I heard rumors and reports of the master, hanging off the after rail, scared to death that he would die and afraid that he wouldn't. I heard him moan as the vessel pitched and I saw him writhing on the deck. I had one of the deck hands lash a line on his leg so we wouldn't lose the body. Other than that, we picked up the sea buoy off St. Petersburg soon after dark and were safe in Tampa Harbor by midnight.

As we prepared to tie up in the near reaches of the harbor, I became conscious of peremptory orders being issued left and right. In the relative calm of Tampa Bay, the captain had come to life. I bowed out. It was interesting to watch. The captain was a stranger to the sea. The only prior encounter he'd had with deep water was as a summer sailor on the lakes. He tied the vessel up with no consideration for the rise and fall of the tide, so we either got hung up in the ebb and wrenched the deck bitts from their bolts or we came near capsizing with the flow. Whatever jeopardy we encountered in that remarkably able sea boat was always at the dock. But that was his department and I never interfered.

At sea, Captain Lawrence took to his bunk. We made port without incident, at which point the master took over. "I told them," he said in a sudden burst of candor, "I told them at the office, either you put Richards back aboard my vessel or I'll walk off." The powers that be capitulated. It would have been a bad day for the Army to lose a man like Lawrence, all of which didn't do me a bit of harm. Now, if I could only navigate. Against the kind of competition I saw, becoming a skipper would be a lead-pipe cinch. I tried to get Captain Lawrence to teach me how. We had a sextant, a chronometer, a Bowditch, a Nautical Almanac, and a copy of H.O. 216 aboard. But if it was a mystery to me, it was a mystery wrapped in an enigma to Larry. He had cribbed his way to captaincy. I began to look elsewhere.

On the passage from Tampa to Key West along the coast we had a dead calm day. The captain rose from his sickbed and came out on deck with the sextant. He pretended to take a shot of the sun. Huddled with his books for three hours, he came up with a latitude roughly on a line with Labrador. I began to study *The American Practical Navigator*. The theory of mathematics fascinated me. The practice of it put me to sleep. Bowditch, with its fancy terms and dead-end alleys, was a powerful soporific. It was better than sleeping pills. Safe, too. You couldn't take an overdose.

It was in Key West that I ran across a book that promised to open Pandora's Box of celestial navigation. I spotted it in a bookstore and, in the spirit of my new found affluence as first officer, I plunked down five bucks and bought it. It was called *Mathematics for the Millions*. If a million could dig it, why not little me? The author was a Britisher by the name of Lancelot Hogben.

Old Lancelot and I got chummy right off. His contention was that from the beginning of time man has used his knowledge to exploit and subjugate his fellow men. That was putting it on a bitter basis. I preferred to believe that man has always used knowledge to get ahead and that it would be a sad day when they changed the name of the game.

With Hogben by my side, the latitude by meridian altitude was duck soup. I was tempted to teach it to the captain, but war is war and to the victor belong the spoils. I borrowed the sextant before noon, took a sight of the sun at its apex, applied the declination for the day from the Nautical Almanac, the corrections for semidiameter, height of eye and parallax, subtracted the result from ninety degrees and marked our position on the chart. The "old man" was too sick to care.

His triumph had come, as it must to all pretty men, in the wonderful world of love. We had gone ashore together in Key West. Old Murphy lit out for a rum joint. I like sugar in any form, fermented or otherwise. I followed Larry into a drug store. We ordered two chocolate sodas.

It was a super drug store. It had everything, including a babe behind the seltzer spigot with a form of such proportions as to border on the grotesque.

She had a special fillup for Larry. She accepted his invitation. He stared at her in disbelief. She met him after closing time and they went off into the night, arm in arm. Larry was near swooning in the contemplation of his good fortune. He opportuned the maiden in the soft moonlight along the strand. He trembled in anticipation as she gently brushed him off in the lonely seclusion of the shrubbery. He was alternately resolute in his demands and a supplicant in dire need. She played cat and mouse with him all over Key West.

When, in the wee hours of the morning, he finally despaired, she led him coyly to the home of her parents and in the syncopation of their snores, with only a bamboo curtain between the lovers and a possible parental paroxysm, she delivered herself forthwith. Larry couldn't believe that it was happening to him. Such beauty, such billow, such bounty. At last they parted. It was dawn and it was war, and the magic of reality dissolved in the earthy evanescence of dream. At ten the captain rose from his lonely pilothouse bunk.

When he came back at noon with his Navy orders, Captain Lawrence was a new man. He was brisk and positive. Once the stores were aboard he gave orders to embark, and we stood out to sea.

It was a slow struggle, man against the sea; but as it had before the sea triumphed. The captain went retching to the rail and, in his delicate condition, clean overboard. But as we got a line around him and hauled him out of the tepid waters of the Gulf Stream and back on board, there was hardly a ripple of mirth from the crew to mar a reputation so solidly achieved.

6

I liked Larry. Larry was a nice clean-cut American boy. How he ever became captain of the T45 was one of the worst-kept secrets of World War II. His father was a friend of the assistant crewing director.

Larry came from the Middle West. He was a well-built guy with an accordian smile. He had brown, wavy hair. In his blue uniform with its gold stripe, he looked exactly as a young American naval officer is supposed to look. But he didn't know a damn thing about the sea.

The girls were crazy about him.

So was everybody else he met when he went ashore. Everybody but the Navy brass. If he hadn't been a Merchant Marine officer they would have slammed him into the brig. Merchant Marine officers like Captain Lawrence were seagoing civilians. They were volunteers. An honest mistake on their part was just one of those things. Larry's sin was to allow the T45 to come into Key West unrecognized. It burned the Navy port director. You just don't bring a vessel into a strategic Navy port like Key West on the sly. Not in time of war. Larry had an excuse.

He was seasick.

He was too seasick to signal his arrival at the sea buoy. He was too seasick to get up and report to the Navy office even after the vessel was docked. He was bad sick. It was a bad thing.

If it got around that you could get seasick and bring a vessel into Key West unbeknownst, it wouldn't be long before the enemy would start hanging over the rail pretending to snap their cookies while they sashayed into harbor with a vessel loaded with TNT. Regurgitation is an ancient diversionary tactic.

With the captain it was the real thing. No one hated it more than he did. All he knew was that the horror of passage from New Orleans was behind him. He knew also that there would be more rolling, more pitching, more agony at the rail. He breathed a curse on a stomach that had turned this "once in a lifetime" voyage into an endless nightmare.

He couldn't wait to get his feet on dry land. As soon as he was out of sight of sea, it was heaven. It was hell, too. The hell was from the Navy and the heaven was from everybody else. Captain Larry became the darling of the Caribbean.

I did the work.

I tried to be a friend, but it was no dice. If I couldn't share his agony at sea, he would be damned if he would share the euphoria of being a skipper ashore. I became a kind of a father to Larry, and you just don't take a daddy on a date. You do take grandma. At least some did in Havana.

Draped across the bulwark on the starboard quarter, his elbows on the rail and his hands holding his head, Larry prayed for instant after-life and to hell with the glories of the flesh. The elements were unconcerned. The wind blew like crazy out of the east. The sea cavorted. The T45 walloped her way across the Straits of Florida, taking the turbulence in her stride.

The Gulf Stream was blood blue in the red rays of the afternoon sun. Torn cloud fragments webbed the sky and the wind reared waves crested across the counter as the little

41

vessel lifted to the surge, sliced the lace of foam and rushed with the combers that tumbled before her. As it set, the sun shot blades of light toward the point of destination. Our southeast course proved perfect. We picked up the double glint from the beacon on the fort as the day was drawn into the west.

The city came up out of the curve of distance. It lay before us heavy with history. The necklace of old buildings on the bay, dusted with the patina of time and burnished by the last light, glowed like a banked fire. The massive rock and abutment of Morro Castle rose above us on the left as a tiny pilot boat came out of nowhere, and the Cuban pilot swung aboard. He took the wheel in the darkness as the T45 entered harbor. We moved along the channel that paralleled the Malecon, alive with lights, and the little vessel fetched up at the government wharf.

We went for the captain aft, hoisted him to his feet, and propped him up against the deck house so that he could sign

the voucher for the pilot. Then we dropped him and went ashore. All of us.

Havana was a swinging town in a world at war. Most of the action swung around the bar in the big hotel on the square. There were girls and rhumba music and all the rum in the world at soda-pop prices. There hadn't been a tourist in Havana for months.

The natives were friendly. The girls were enthusiastic. A date with one of those girls was like a short-term marriage. Once you made your choice you had better stick with it. The girls battled for their rights to a man with everything they had. Wiles, fingernails, invective, and, if need be, the jagged edge of a broken bottle. It was a new kind of world.

The captain dragged himself out of his pilothouse cocoon as we drifted back, one by one, to the mother ship in the morning. It was near noon when he picked up his cap, the ship's secret documents, and headed for the Navy office.

It was springtime and Havana. The combination got him. The old world buildings beckoned. The wide park with its great trees and noble monuments sparkled like a pointillistic painting in the sunlight. Larry wandered far afield. The Navy would have to wait. Somewhere on the *Paseo Del Prado* a dark-eyed senorita drew a bead on him through slow-descending eyelashes. Larry dallied. He lost his steerage like a disabled ship. Larry was taken in tow. She took him home with her as a prize. Mamma mia adored him. Papa Pedro shook his hand. He was offered sanctuary. He was presented with the possibility of a big job on the sugar plantation. Larry was on a collision course with matrimony.

In this peaceful little planet, flung off like a fragment from a world at war and occupied with its own orbit, anything could happen and often did. There was a sudden celebration. There were food and wine and cousins and kin. There was laughter and talk and a high-keyed gaiety, all in Spanish of which Larry knew nary a word. He had been taken up by one of the first families of Havana.

43

It didn't figure. Larry had to get alone with this lovely little Latin and ask some questions. But first he had to get back the classified ship's papers and the secret code that were being passed from cousin to uncle and from nephew to aunt as positive proof that this young, handsome, smiling gringo was, in fact, the master of a United States vessel.

Larry got the papers back. Then he got the doll and got away. But not completely. Grandma came along. They went dancing in the park with grandma holding the papers, and they sat sipping sodas in the rotunda with the uncompromising matrona standing by, ready to blow the whistle. There was no conversation. It was hard to evaluate the situation. It occurred to the captain that it wasn't practicable. He borrowed the papers for a moment and blew.

I got the whole story when I ran into him on Neptuna Boulevard, on his way to the Navy office. We went into the Plaza for a drink. It was late afternoon, and the action had slowed after last night's rumpus. There was no one besides us in the place, except the bartender and the lady in charge of entertainment, who was very sociable, mostly on account of Larry.

"Are you the captain of the ship?" she asked for a starter. Larry looked at me and agreed tentatively.

"So young and so handsome," said Madam Marta.

"Aren't all captains young and handsome?" I asked. "But not like thees one," then, turning to Larry, "Would you like to have a good job?"

"The captain has a good job."

"Ah, but not like thees job." Marta shifted her 180 pounds of femininity closer to Larry. "What do you say, Capitan? Plenty money, plenty rum, and any girl in the house."

Larry was stunned. He turned pale and glassy eyed. He searched around for an out. The old sickness was on him again. For Larry, the terrors of the sea were as nothing compared to the jeopardy of the land. He stumbled toward the door.

I caught up with him at the curb. He waited while I went

back to the table and picked up the ship's classified papers, then we hopped a taxi to the ship. The Navy could wait.

We caught a glimpse of her sheer, half-curtained by the grey sails of a Cuban fisherman, as the cab coughed along the wharf. We saw her long, low profile through a web of fish nets drying in the evening sunlight. She had grace and balance and the beam of an able lady. We stepped from the old pier to her deck and passed beneath the boom that stretched aft from her stubby mast and was chocked above the pilothouse. Larry said, hopefully, "I bet we could rig her with the awning as a steadying sail."

She was a nice home to come back to. I knew that he hated himself for all the woe she brought him. He stepped up to the pilothouse, sacked out, and lost himself in sleep. I climbed back on the wharf for another look at the little 65-foot vessel that carried a strange cargo of mixed motives.

The captain loved the tiny ship. Conway, the gung-ho chief, was an Australian. He wanted to help win the war. If there was a buck in it, all the better. Jonesy, his assistant, longed to be a hero. He longed even more for home and his girl in Cleveland. The two deck hands were out to beat the draft. Getting blasted out of the water or drowned in the process was unthinkable. Bill, the cook, went along. He had cast himself in the role of a Texas badman, but suffered the indignity of woman's work, waiting silently for the provocation to blast away. I sat on the caprail of the weathered wharf as the sun went down, watching the fishing vessels come in among the long shadows. I wondered how brave I'd be if the chips were down.

The crew drifted back to the T45 early. They were broke now and ready to sail. In the morning, the captain went to the Navy office for his orders. The Navy commander looked at him unbelieving. "Now where in hell have you been?" he asked. It was a good question.

We shoved off, with orders to take the vessel to Panama. What more could a young guy ask for?

"A decent stomach, that's what," growled Larry.

We came into Bahia Honda in the afternoon. The sea was so calm that you could have played Kelly pool on the hatch cover. Larry came out of the everlasting bout with his belly and took command of the T45. The outline of hills lay to the left, with the steeple of the church showing above a tangle of green. According to the chart and the sailing directions, the channel ran southeast, close aboard a reef that swung out from the west.

We were headed west. The steeple was not yet on our port beam. "Run her in," said the master.

"Larry, you'll run her aground."

"Why?"

"The channel runs in a southeasterly direction."

"I don't see any shoal water. Run her in," said Captain Lawrence.

"You'll tear the bottom out of her."

"Run her in," said the captain.

"Here's the wheel," I said, "you run her in. I'll go sit in the lifeboat." I stepped out of the pilothouse, climbed to the boat deck and got into the lifeboat.

The captain leaned out of the pilothouse door. "Mr. Richards," he roared.

"Yes Sir," I said.

"Come back in here."

"Yes Sir," I said. I came down, took the wheel, and put her head west. I kept a running patter going like a vaudeville magician while the vessel edged along.

"I don't see why we can't run right in," said the captain.

"You see, Larry, it's like finding your way around a strange town. The channel into a harbor is like the main drag. You've got to walk down Forty-Second Street to get to Fifth Avenue. Fifth Avenue is the main drag."

"I've never been to New York," said Larry.

"Where are you from?"

"Chicago."

"Haven't they got a main drag in that city?"

"Yeah, but it swings around."

"I've never been to Chicago," I said.

When the steeple showed to the southeast across the compass card, I turned her head and ran her in. We passed close aboard the reef, and we watched in silence as the sea broke gently on the coral shoals at the point. Once we were past the reef, Bahia Honda opened up into a lovely anchorage. The bay stretched for a mile up to the edge of a little Cuban village. Larry and the crew went ashore in the dinghy. I stayed aboard. I had some letters to write.

I sat in the pilothouse. It was hot. The windows were the kind that you lower into a well in the bulkhead. You've got to watch your fingers when you let them down. I didn't. I caught the third finger of my left hand, wedged tight between the top of the window and the sill. I couldn't get it out. It hurt. I mean hurt. There I stood, with my finger caught in a trap like a wild animal, and not a soul in sight. It was too far from land to yell for help. The whistle cord was just beyond my reach. It might be hours before the crew came back. The sun beat down. I agonized.

There was no way to get the window up with one hand and I had nothing to pry it with. I cursed the builder, the marine architect, and my own damn foolishness. I struggled and strained to no avail. I was careless and I was caught. I was going to have to sweat it out till the crew returned.

Suddenly I saw a figure on the dock, a half mile away. It looked as though it might be the captain. He got into the dinghy and started rowing out to the vessel. Took his time about it, too.

It was the captain. He came alongside at last and jumped up on the deck. He said, "I've come to get you." I was numb.

"How about getting this window off my finger?" He came into the pilothouse and pulled the strap that lifted the window. I was free.

"I found the greatest eating place in town," said Larry. "I didn't want you to miss it. The most marvelous food you ever

47

tasted." We got into the dinghy. The captain rowed as he went on about the food. "Fish and lobster and meat and sauces, all being cooked in a garden over a charcoal fire. They cook it in cast-iron shells. I caught a whiff of it half across the town. Guess how much it costs?"

I was in no condition to venture a guess.

"Only thirteen cents," he said. "Can you imagine a full meal for thirteen cents?" He rowed in silence across the tranquil bay.

"Larry," I said, "why did you come back to get me?"

"Well," he said, "there was this bunch of Cuban fishermen in that eating place. I told them that I was the captain. I don't think they believed me. They laughed."

"You *are* kind of young," I said.

"I want you to tell them," he said with the smile.

"I'll tell them," I said, "I'll tell them."

I told them in Bahia Honda. I told them in Cozumel. I told them in Puerto Castilla and Puerto Cabezas. I told them in Limón. I told them all the way to Panama. With Captain Lawrence seasick as hell and hanging over the after bulwark with one hand frozen on the flagstaff while he was snapping his cookies, the natives were hard to convince.

Nonetheless, I was as good as my word. I told them.

The crew began to join in the game. They told them too. When a pilot came aboard and asked for the captain as they invariably do, the crew took a fiendish delight in pointing him out.

"The captain? You will find him on the afterdeck hanging on to the flagpole. He is having a little navigation problem. Perhaps you had better talk to the mate."

When we brought the little ship into Panama Harbor, we tied her up alongside the Gatun Locks. Larry hit the sack for twenty-four hours before he reported his arrival to the Navy.

When Captain Lawrence walked in and announced his arrival, the officer of the watch was stricken with panic. The T45 had come in without signaling its secret code identifica-

tion. She had been lying for twenty-four hours alongside the .
most vital and vulnerable mechanism in all of World War II.

If she had been an enemy vessel in disguise and loaded
with TNT, that would have been the end of the Panama
Canal and the end of everything. A disaster like that would
have taken the heart out of the war effort.

Back in New Orleans a gentleman by the name of
Placaides had a similar problem.

7

Mr. Placaides sat and listened to his heart. This was something new for Mr. Placaides. Mr. Placaides had never listened to his heart before. Mr. Placaides was a banker, and a banker cannot afford to listen to his heart. Certainly not if he wishes to stay in business.

Just the same, Mr. Placaides listened to his heart because it said a very important thing to him. It said that he, Placaides, was going to die.

Mr. Placaides would not have believed his heart if he had not fallen down with a great pain in it the day before. When the pain went away, he knew that henceforth he would have to listen to his heart.

It made Placaides the banker sad. "Venus," he said.

His wife turned and showed her profile. "Yes, Ben."

"I am listening to my heart."

"Yes, Ben."

"It does not tell me a good thing."

"The doctor said that you should rest."

"How can a man rest who listens to his heart?"

Mrs. Placaides did not answer. She turned her head away and ironed the wrinkles from the lap of her gown with her palm, reached out with her free hand, and touched the hand of Virgilio Varga who sat next to her in the shadow.

Varga took her hand in his and squeezed. He squeezed tightly thinking of the way this woman did the very same for him. He had never known such a woman. All his life he had searched for a woman like this, and now he must leave her. All because of a war.

"When do you sail, Varga?" said Mr. Placaides.

"I do not know."

"You are welcome here," said Placaides.

"I am very grateful," said Varga.

"It is nothing."

It became night. The light in the kitchen was turned off, and the cook passed them sitting there. She did not speak. Venus Placaides called after her to wish her well, and she acknowledged the wish with a little bow, closing the garden door behind her.

"It is time," said Venus Placaides.

"Another moment," said Ben Placaides.

"It is past the hour."

"I wish to hold this time. I am afraid."

"Of what?"

"I am afraid of the bed."

Varga squeezed the hand of Venus Placaides in the dark. He was not afraid of the bed. He was not afraid of the old man. He was afraid only of the war. He was afraid that the vast sin that possessed the world would blow this curious constellation to hell and gone.

There was little hate in the heart of Virgilio Varga. There was love. Even for the old man. Varga was sure that the old man knew, and because of some dim twist of memory, he was glad.

Varga knew too that the old man had come to the stern conclusion that he, Señor Placaides, must never again have this woman who was his own wife. There was a reason.

Varga knew the reason. He knew it from the very first

moment that he was locked in her embrace. There simply was no release. Not unless she wished it so. Varga knew that there were few women so endowed. In all his life he had never known of such a woman. Watching the old man in the shadows, Varga tried to feel for a moment the fierce love of being alive that must move the old man.

To have such a woman and not have her. To relinquish such a woman. Would not that be the same as death? To Varga, it was beyond understanding. Suddenly, this man sitting in the shadows appeared to Varga as his own father. And then, just as quickly, it was as if this woman he loved was his dead mother. Now suddenly, he longed for the possessive thing that is in all women. The thing that lies at the beginning of eternal pain. The involuntary contraction of the sphincter, against which is pitted the endless will to be born.

"Perhaps if you had delivered yourself of a child," said Varga softly to Señora Placaides.

Venus, dimly divining the flow of his thoughts, bowed her head in a gesture of assent and held his hand even more tightly.

"Then perhaps you would have learned something that would help me now, so that I may go forth."

Venus looked at him, turning her head slowly, and a pain like a flash of false labor pressed against her diaphragm. For a long moment her breath would not return, and she released her hold on Varga's hand; and just as quickly in Varga there was a fierce lust to be held, a lust to be held for good, to be held against the encroachment of time and death, to be held against the engulfment of war, of the sea, of the unutterable aloneness that only this woman, since the day of his passage into the world, could allay.

In the darkness the bent figure of Ben Placaides rose and moved along the garden wall. Quietly Venus left the side of Varga and walked with Ben Placaides to the door of the old brick house. Together they went in. Varga sat alone in the darkness and waited, falling asleep at last on the padded settee in the shadows.

She came to Varga in the small hours of the morning. She stood with her back to him watching the three stars that form the belt of Orion as they disentangled themselves from the iron filigree. She turned, knelt on the soft turf alongside of where he lay sleeping. Then she bowed her head as if in prayer and kissed his eyes. First one, then the other.

He drew her down upon himself and she whispered, "Virgilio, Virgilio, I am sick with fear."

Varga opened his eyes and saw the fear in her face. He said, "Are you afraid for me?"

"No," she said, "I am afraid for myself." She buried her head beneath his chin.

"Why?"

"There will be a time when I will be unable to let you go."

"I live for that hour." Varga parted her robe and moved his hand held flat across the face of her breast, feeling the stiff tissue of her teat as it described a tiny circle in his palm. Venus shivered and groped for his tongue in hunger. They turned a half circle in the deepness of the shadows, and he moved slowly in upon her, timing each stage of his entrance to the pulsations of her need, while the jowls of her vulva took irrevocable possession of his person.

They lay motionless, locked in the tight adaptation of their desire, helplessly aware of a door that opened and then, at last, of a door that closed.

Virgilio Varga walked away from the house on Marion Street, from that last tenuous release down through the musty fragrance of the old quarter. The night was dusted with the distillate of magnolia must, and the wind, coming far in from the sea, mixed its sweet smells with the aromatics of the Bayou country. Varga climbed the embankment along the Industrial Canal, feeling the tender leaves of grass with the tips of his fingers; he strode along the concrete wall and came hesitantly aboard the ST250 just as someone said, "Aw, bullshit!"

There was a long silence. Virgilio stood in the galley door balancing his sea bag on one shoulder. His eyes moved deliberately from Texas to Reinecke, from Reinecke to Cork, and from Cork to the chief engineer.

Cork put a hot cup of coffee down on the galley table, pointed to the chief and said, "This bastard claims he knows a squaw up on Marion Street who has a muscle that can hang onto your wang till you say 'Uncle.' "

"Bullshit," said Texas.

8

It was hard to believe that Virgilio Varga was for real. Not that I worried about it; I had enough on my mind before I became the master of the ST250. I had signed on a gasoline tanker as first officer. Varga was a deck hand on my watch.

One night when we were on the bridge, he prattled away about some kind of a savant who was the professor of philosophy at the University of Salamanca during the Spanish Inquisition. It seems that this bird was shooting off his mouth to the students, one of whom was a Christ-bitten bastard who turned him in.

Arrested by the Church authorities, the professor was tried by the Court of the Inquisition and sentenced to twenty years in solitary confinement.

"Can you imagine," said Varga, his peepers popping out at me, "twenty years of solitary confinement?"

I leaned on the bulwark and stared out through the maze of rigging at the glow of lights in New Orleans. It was hard to imagine. I wondered whether twenty years of solitary confinement was worse or better than being blown to hell in a split second by a high-octane tanker.

Varga's eyes went back into their respective caves under

that shaggy brow. "After twenty years they sprang him. He returned to his classroom. And," said Virgilio with the eyes coming out of those caves again, "his opening remark to his students was, 'As I was saying yesterday.'"

You don't often run into guys like Varga going to sea. I knew all about his design for living with that acrobatic female up on Marion Street and her moribund old man, but this sudden revelation of the liberal side of his nature had me taking another look at him.

There wasn't much to look at. He walked with a shuffle like a gorilla, and he did a lot of staring into space. One night I went to my cabin to turn in, and I found him asleep in my bunk.

"What the hell are you doing here?"

"Sleeping," he said, "It's cooler up here than down in the foc'sle."

I threw the bum out on his ear. I didn't hold it against him. As a matter of fact, I liked him. Where else were you going to find anybody you could talk to on any subject beside women, loot, or the imminence of disaster?

The tanker had been fabricated in Texas. Her name was Y19. She was a hundred-and-ten-foot-high octane tanker designed to carry aviation gasoline to the South Pacific Islands. She lay in drydock in the sweltering heat of summer in New Orleans. The shipyard gang was climbing all over her, reworking her fittings with acetylene torches. Every time a door slammed or a port banged closed I thought she was about to blow sky-high.

The old man was absent-minded as hell. He was so concerned that the ship would explode that he seemed at times to have lost his buttons. When the ship left Port Arthur, he left the classified ship's papers on a piling at the dock.

Somebody had to go back and get them. The captain's job was at stake. I volunteered. I would have volunteered for the landing at D-day. Anything to get off that trap.

The old man nosed her into a mud bank. I climbed down a

56

rope ladder from the bow and sank waist deep in the bog. I struggled out to the highway, covered with mud, and started thumbing my way back to Port Arthur.

Cars were few and far between. I poured the water out of my shoes and started hoofing. A fellow came along and gave me a ride for a couple of miles. He saw the mud on my pants and dumped me.

Cars went by without stopping. There was damn little enthusiasm for the war in Louisiana. Most of the eligible men in the parishes had figured a way to beat the draft. They signed up as deputy sheriffs.

A fellow came along with a fancy-looking babe in the seat beside him. "Hop in," he said. I took a seat in the back of the car, and we headed for Port Arthur. It was a long drive.

The babe in the front seat started talking about her husband. His name was Harry. She was obviously wild about Harry.

The driver agreed wholeheartedly. "Harry is a wonderful guy. He is a great friend of mine."

They had something in common. An abiding admiration for Harry. "Remember the time in Port Neches when Harry wore the silk topper to the oyster roast, and Rufus shot a hole through it. Wasn't that a scream?"

"Yeah," said the driver, "Harry is a wonderful guy. Remember how Margie screamed when Harry slipped a fish in her boot?"

I dozed off listening to all the wonderful things about Harry. I had been walking, riding, walking all day in a wet suit, and I was bushed.

I flaked out in the back seat for the better part of two hours. When I woke the driver and the babe were snuggled in a clinch, evidently attracted to each other by their mutual admiration for Harry.

The driver interrupted his petting and his driving long enough to look back and say, "We are making a turn at the next light. Do you want to get off?"

"Thanks," I said, "I'd like that." I got out and closed the door of the car, saying, "Give my regards to Harry."

They took off like a drag racer.

Port Arthur was only a couple of miles away. I found the classified ship's papers in a briefcase still perched on a piling at the end of the dock. I grabbed it and started back. It was getting dark.

I must have walked ten miles with cars passing me every few minutes. At last I saw a bus coming up the road. Surely he would stop. I stepped out into the middle of the road and waved the briefcase. It had to stop or run me down.

The bus careened by on the left side of the road, missing my head by inches. Now it was getting quite dark, and I was out in the bush. Still the cars went by. Getting a ride at night was impossible. I saw a light on the side of the road ahead. I kept walking.

It was a tavern. I walked in. There were a lot of men around a big table covered with green felt. A crap game was in full swing. A guy in a sharp business suit was faded and crapped out. I walked up to him and told him about the ship's papers and my predicament.

"O.K." he said, "I'm going that way. I'll give you a lift. Wait till I get my money back."

I waited. The war waited. The man kept on shooting craps. I waited all night. The war waited all night. The man kept winning and losing till seven o'clock in the morning.

At last he turned to me and said, "O.K., I'm broke. Let's go."

I walked aboard the Y19 at noon. I handed the briefcase with the ship's papers to the captain.

He took them and said, "Very well."

It was a hell of a way to thank me. I became more determined than ever to pack in the Y19.

At the moment it didn't seem possible. If a guy went crying to the shipping office they would figure that he was windy, and they would keep him on that trap forever.

The very next day I got my chance.

Word gets around fast in a place like a port of embarkation. I had saved the captain's hide by going back and finding those papers. He wasn't about to mention that little favor to the shipping director, but it was twenty-to-one that somebody else would.

The tanker had been hauled, and they were busy painting her bottom. To make things even more delirious, they were loading her up with high-octane aviation gasoline.

I decided to cut down the chances of being blown to hell by taking a walk. It was a pretty day. There were little clouds in the sky heading north as if they had some place to go. I had no place to go. All I wanted to do was to get away from that bomb. I gravitated to the shipping office down at the Port of Embarkation.

I took a deep breath and walked into the old man's office with a smile on my face and the most casual manner I could muster. "Higgins," I said, with my foot up on his desk, "Haven't you got a ship that goes to sea? I'm burned out on hanging around a shipyard."

He looked up at me over his bifocals. "It just so happens that I have. There is a captain down in Key West with a large tug and a barge. He has been hiring and firing mates, trying to come up with a navigator. He has been running aground all over the place. He's an old tugboat man from Tampa. Got his license over there. Probably stole it. Go down there and help him take that layout to Panama. I was wondering who in hell to send down there."

By nightfall I was on a plane headed east and saying to myself, "who in hell to send down there . . . who in hell to send down there."

"Did you say something?" It was the stewardess. She was a doll.

"Yeah," I said. "Do you ever worry about dying?"

"Can't afford to on this job."

"Like to have a drink with me when we get to Jacksonville?"

· "I'd love it."

"Where will I met you?"

"Somebody is meeting me. But if he doesn't show . . ."

He showed. I spent the night alone in a motel in Jacksonville, hopped a bus to Key West in the morning and joined the vessel at noon.

It was one of the powerful and steady 105-foot Army Transport tugs, and she had an enormous steel barge lying alongside. The captain's name was Lawson. He knew how to handle a tug in a harbor, which is no small accomplishment, but out at sea he got the shakes. He never knew where he was. Tampa was a rough town. You could buy anything there. He bought his license.

We were still in sight of the sea buoy after we left Key West when the captain came charging up to me, his eyes blazing. "Where are we?"

He wanted an immediate demonstration of my ability as a navigator. I pointed at the sea buoy and paid him no mind.

It was a hectic voyage, with the old man hanging over me every minute wanting to know where we were. It was overcast as we bucked the Gulf Stream, turned the corner at the western tip of Cuba and headed down along Cozumel. There was no way of getting a shot of the sun or a star. It began to drive the old man nuts. We had to run dead reckoning, and with a hawser whip sawing on the fantail, it was impossible to string a log.

At noon the third day out I caught a lucky sight of the sun and got a meridian altitude. With a known latitude we were able to pick up a lighthouse on the Honduranian coast and make port on the Nicaraguan shore in the late afternoon.

Puerto Cabezas was a crummy little town with a row of shanties along a drainage ditch that served as a sewer, a barroom up on a hill, with a long unpainted wooden awning and a donkey tethered to one of the stanchions that supported it.

Inside the place there was a mud floor, a bar with a washtub alongside it, half-full of bottles of beer and a chunk of ice. There were no lights and no electricity. God only knows where that lonely little piece of ice came from.

The barkeeper was all smiles when the crew piled in. It was a lopsided smile that disclosed four discolored teeth on the starboard side, with one that sported a gold cap, and no teeth at all on the port side. He bent over and started opening the beer bottles.

I took my beer out and sat on a wooden crate under the makeshift awning and looked down through the sparse, tangled growth of mahogany and trumpet vines at the poor little gardens and the lopsided one-room shacks. This was what we call "poor-ass country." I thought about the war and the vicious extravagance of it.

There was a whisper of a breeze coming in off the lagoon and a young woman coming up the hill. Her hair was tied in a ponytail with a soiled little yellow ribbon. Her cotton shirt had a frayed lace collar and her skirt was tied around her tiny waist with a length of cord out of which was woven the fishnet that hung from the rafters. She stood there smiling at me while she ran her palm along the furry flank of the donkey. She was what is known down there as a "public woman."

We went together into a little room that adjoined the bar. That room had a specific function. The only furniture was a dilapidated bed. There wasn't even a door, just a curtain separating it from the barroom. She was kind of coy taking off her shirt and untying her skirt. She had no shoes.

The slanting sunlight coming through the single-shuttered window fell in tiger stripes across her firm brown breasts and her slender thighs. Her eyes were luminous and smokey, and her teeth flashed white. I sat on the bed beside her saying to myself, "So this is a public woman."

61

Rolling a condom on I tried to lighten the tension by translating the motto of the Boy Scouts of America into Spanish. She didn't know what the hell I was talking about. She smiled and pulled me toward her. She didn't want to kiss me.

Her legs parted and locked behind me vehemently. Now it was warm and tight and pulsating. I was drawn deep into those tender folds, which are like sea flowers that caress the stringent tide. It was long and slow, and I flowed at last into a bottomless abyss.

She was spent and I was spent. I looked down along the undulations of her nakedness unbelieving. As long as she remained a "public woman," the public had a lot to be thankful for.

She lay with her head resting on my arm and suddenly her face grew tense as the curtain moved. She indicated that the guys in the bar had been peeking in during the entire performance. I got dressed, slipped her an extra couple of bucks, and went out into the barroom.

The peeping toms were all charged up. I had another beer and stood at the bar watching them as they gyrated around the room, generally tearing the place up.

When the "public woman" got dressed, she came out and stood next to me at the bar. When she was approached by any of the crew she spat at them. Most of the crew rushed down to where the tug was moored and plunged into the sea. It cooled them off, but they came out hollering with pain. For miles along that coast the shoreline is infested with nettles. The captain went into hiding.

The rest of the voyage to Panama was uneventful. The crew was subdued and the old man stayed in his corner. He came alive when we lost the barge right in the channel that led to the entrance of the canal.

The captain did a great job rescuing that behemoth of a barge before it drifted off into shoal water. I had to hand it to him. He knew how to handle a tug. But in the process of catching up with the fast drifting barge, he dragged a five-hundred-pound shackle at the end of a couple hundred yards of steel cable all through the mine field that guards the canal. I was waiting to be blown out of the water.

It never happened. I found out later that all those mines are controlled from a station on the shore. I don't know whether the captain knew it or not. We had very little to say to each other. He looked so happy at being able to demonstrate what he did know that he never gave the mines a thought. We tied up the barge in the Panama harbor, and in the morning we headed back for New Orleans.

The weather was fair, with a gentle breeze out of the south. We had been informed in Panama that the lighthouse at Cabo Gracias à Dios which stands half-way through Miskitos Channel on the Nicaraguan coast, had been shelled by a Nazi submarine and was no longer operational. Miskitos Channel is the one treacherous passage on the most direct route from Panama to New Orleans. It stretches for forty-five miles studded with coral pinnacles, all marked on the chart, that can tear the bottom out of a vessel.

Running light and with a favorable current, we were doing better than 17 knots. We approached Miskitos Channel at eight o'clock in the evening. The course was set dead center of the channel. I went below and turned in.

I was just drifting off, lulled by the easy pitching motion of the vessel, when suddenly the pitching motion became a rolling motion. The tug had changed course. I looked at my watch. It was nine o'clock. We were less than halfway through the channel, right abeam of the lighthouse on the cape.

I pulled on my pants and went up to the wheelhouse. Martinez, the second mate, was at the wheel. He was from Tampa too. I peered over his shoulder into the binnacle. We were heading for the coral pinnacles.

"Who put you on this course?"

"The captain," he said defiantly.

"You are headed straight for the beach. You had better change course and head north."

"No way," said Martinez.

"You are putting her on the rocks."

"Look," said Martinez, "The captain gave me this course, and this is the course I steer."

We had scarcely ten minutes before we would surely fetch up on that jagged reef. I went down below to the captain's cabin and rapped gently on the door. I heard him grunt and wheeze. "What do you want?" he demanded.

"Captain, I don't like to bother you, but there is something I don't understand about the chart. I wonder if you would explain it to me."

In a manner fraught with supplication and self-effacement, I managed to entice him out to the chart table.

"We have been running this channel for one hour. We are moving at the rate of 17 knots. We left here at eight o'clock." The second point of the dividers came down due east of the lighthouse. "Assuming we are right here . . ."

Suddenly the captain was up the companionway like a cat with a bulldog on his tail. He swung her back on course. Then he came back down and invited me into his cabin where he proceeded to relate a pattern of hardships, family woes, and broken friendships, ending with a tearful plea for me not to mention this incident to the shipping director in New Orleans.

I looked at this weeping, peeping tom with the bold braid on his visor.

I promised.

Nonetheless, he was out in the wheelhouse in the morning with the same nasty vilification of my proficiency as a navigator. Now he could afford to be cocky. There were no more reefs between what had been "Cape Grace of God" and New Orleans. He could make home port without me.

Virgilio Varga handled the problem of getting separated from that high octane tanker more directly. He simply walked off the ship. What he did was tantamount to desertion. He was discharged from the Army Transport Service, blackballed by the War Shipping Administration, and rendered vulnerable to the draft.

Then he hit the bottle.

Poor Varga was caught between the ferocious clutch of Señora Placaides and the voracious gnawing of the demon rum. The only possible escape from that dual jeopardy was to go to sea. There was no way. He was down in a bar near the Port of Embarkation, swilling bourbon and ruminating on his predicament, which, in his misty thinking, was not unlike the kind of a bind that the professor at Salamanca had found himself in.

It was a hot, muggy day in New Orleans. I had been living at the Hotel Monteleon for a month, painting. I had gotten a letter from the White House signed by Major General Watson, aide to President Roosevelt, saying that the president wished to thank me for my thoughtfulness. I had presented, through the United Seamen's Service, a painting to the president called "Jury Rig." It was a picture of my own little Friendship sloop *Princess,* dismasted in a violent storm trying to make a safe landfall.

The painting symbolized the situation the nation was in after Pearl Harbor. I knew that F.D.R. would dig it. He had been a small boat sailor down east. I happened to show the letter to Colonel Rogers, who was chief of staff at the Port of Embarkation. The upshot of the whole thing was that I was taken off the ships and directed to paint a number of scenes depicting the operations of the Army Transport Service. The paintings were framed in the shop at the port and installed in the Delgado Museum at City Park. The officers' wives had a big wing-ding at the opening. All the brass at the port as well as twenty-one generals who happened to be in New Orleans on a conference attended. So did I. I came with Enrique Alferez and his statuesque wife, Judy.

Ricky was a Mexican sculptor. After standing around unnoticed for half an hour, we could see that the party was a charter flight of ego trips. "C'mon," said Ricky, "these people have no time for you. Don't you know that you are only the artist? Let's get out of here."

We hit a couple of bars on Royal Street and ended up in one down near the Port of Embarkation. Virgilio Varga was there. We bought him a drink and listened to his woes. I thought about Salamanca, the Inquisition, and the old man counting out his days in solitary confinement. "Don't worry Varga," I said, "You'll be back on a ship."

Ricky and Judy blew, and I walked uptown to my room in the hotel. As I passed under the filigree of ironwork and the elaborate balconies of the old French Quarter, I did a lot of thinking.

I was a navigator, but I had no license. I was finding it impossible to continue to argue my way all over the ocean with skippers who didn't know one end of a sextant from the other. The obvious solution was a demotion to the status of able-bodied seaman.

The next day I stated my case to Lew Higgins.

"I guess we will have to send you out as master. Go over to Captain Lord's office and get his O.K. I have a small tug for you to take out to the Pacific.

I waited for Captain Lord in his office. I waited two hours, during which I did a feasibility study of the situation. There were two questions uppermost in my mind.

One—did I want to be the captain of a small, top-heavy tug on a voyage to the Pacific?

Two—did I think that I could make it?

The verdict on both counts was a unanimous and resounding "no." Then why in hell was I waiting for Captain Lord?

I had just about decided to take a powder when Captain Lord walked in. He started off by saying, "Do you have any kind of a license?"

"No."

The captain made a call down to the crewing director.

After he hung up there was a brief hesitation. He tapped his pen on the desk.

"Captain," I said, "this is no goddamn picnic."

The pen in his hand did a one and one-half back dive and came down writing. He signed the authorization. I walked out of there the skipper of the ST250.

Now, as master, I had muscle. I got Ricky, the sculptor, a job as oiler on the ST250, although he had no papers at all, not even citizenship papers. Then I went to Higgins and demanded that they reinstate Virgilio Varga and appoint him to the position of second officer on the ST250.

Higgins looked at me as if I had blown my stack. When you have muscle, you have to exercise it, or you run the danger of losing it. I was brandishing every ounce of muscle I had. Everyone in the crewing office knew that Varga was a dipso and a disaster. Higgins tried to reason with me. I was adamant. He smiled and signed Virgilio Varga on the ST250 as second officer.

He figured that if I could manage Lawson, I could get by with Varga. I could hardly believe what was happening. Evidently, I did have muscle. As master that's what I had to have. Lew Higgins was a smart old country boy.

Looking back, I don't really believe that Higgins thought that I could keep that trap on its feet all the way out to Pearl Harbor. Maybe he figured that if anybody could make it, I could.

I did not share that notion. Neither did the old-time skippers who came down along the catwalk and looked at the vessel. "Pearl Harbor," they said, then shook their heads and walked away.

At first glance, the ST250 appeared to be an able vessel. Despite her short forefoot, she had a lovely sheer and a nicely proportioned deckhouse, with six cabins for the crew. Unlike most tugboats, her galley was amidships.

In all the old-line tugs, the galley was forward, with the curve of the deckhouse providing a place for a big, round table. This created a kind of a family atmosphere. On the ST250 the table was a long board jammed against the forward bulkhead in the midship galley opposite the refrigerator and the stove.

The chief engineer and the two officers in the black gang were quartered in the port cabin aft. The oilers and the cook shared the starboard cabin. The second mate and the rest of the deck crew were forward.

Amidships, port and starboard, there were ladders to the boat deck. Behind the pilothouse there was a small cabin, which was the captain's quarters. There were two bunks in that cabin, one for the captain and the other for the first officer. A door from that cabin led into the pilothouse.

Behind the captain's quarters there was a fidley that opened down into the engine room and a large false stack. The only function of that stack was to make the tug look like an old-time steam job. The exhaust pipe from the engine that it housed was no bigger around than your leg. It did supply a place for the inscription, U.S. ARMY ST250.

On the boat deck, behind the stack, a ten-foot lifeboat fitted with davits lay in chocks. How that lifeboat was supposed to accommodate ten men in an emergency was a mystery only the sanguine bastards in the War Department could propound.

As pretty as she was, the concept of a tugboat rendered completely in steel was a hallucination that could only become a reality when the Army decided to have more seagoing tonnage under its command than the Navy.

Traditionally, a tugboat was constructed so that her weight above the waterline was as light as spruce and plywood could make it. Even if the hull was made of steel, the topsides had to be constructed of light material. Her ballast, which gave her stability, consisted of the engine and her bunkers.

On the ST250 not only was the deckhouse and the whole superstructure made of steel but the mast, which is always spruce on other tugs, was a series of steel pipes in diminishing size, welded together. It was unbelievable and it was deadly.

I could see those monkeys in the drafting room up in Washington. The brass was breathing down their necks saying, "We need a thousand tugs yesterday to draw those oil barges up through the inland waterway. Specify steel. We can get them fabricated in a hurry."

"Yes, sir."

They got them out in a hurry, and they capsized in a hurry.

How many of those jobs went down with all hands was one of the solemn secrets at the Port of Embarkation.

When I stepped aboard her low bulwark, I could actually feel the vessel incline toward me. I couldn't believe it in a boat that weighed close to a hundred tons. The center of gravity must have been up in the wheelhouse. When the rollers came in from a passing ship, she wanted to turn over right at the dock.

She rolled endlessly after the ship passed by. I could break the rhythm of the roll and settle her down by jamming my shoulder against a bulkhead in the wheelhouse at the proper instant. If I did it at the wrong moment, she would roll even more.

That was the vessel we were taking on a five-thousand-mile journey in the open sea. She wasn't fit to go down to the lower bay, but she was my first command and I loved her. I had owned and sailed tender boats all my life, and I was determined that she was not going to catch me napping.

I had no illusions about what it was going to take to get her down to Panama, up the west coast of Central America, and across twenty-four hundred miles of the Pacific. It meant watching the weather like a hawk, and it meant endless tricks at the wheel, unless I could find a quartermaster who had owned a sailboat with no ballast.

There were none. All the sailboat owners were fancy dudes who went into the Navy.

The Navy did all right. They got more equipment and

their aim improved. After a while the submarine menace along the Atlantic seaboard was no longer a factor to be reckoned with. That's when the Army decided to send the tugboats overseas.

9

Long before Tennessee Williams wrote the play, there was a streetcar called "Desire." I boarded it and rode up into the French Quarter. I found Ricky in his studio packing a sea bag. Wherever he went he took along his carving tools and chisels. Judy, his tall blonde wife, was perched on a block of limestone looking at him.

"What do you think of Ricky shipping out to Honolulu?"

"Great," she said with a toothy smile.

Ricky was part Aztec, part Spanish, part black, and brilliant. He had a Van Dyke beard and the body of a black-belt Judo champ. He sparkled.

Ricky was a thoroughly trained academic sculptor. He also had a special talent for getting involved with tall, blonde, blue-eyed females who are so scarce in Mexico as to be considered something of a deity.

They say that this guy was a veritable love machine. After a brief courtship, Ricky would persuade these adventurous gals to hop a bus to the border where they would buy a couple of horses and ride down through the bush to Mexico City. Ricky would enter his home town in triumph with a blonde goddess beside him in a saddle.

71

Most of these babes, however, did not make it. They came down en route with everything from dysentery to crotch itch. They generally wired home to mama for money, and Ricky would return undaunted to New Orleans and pick up another tall, blonde, statuesque tourist. His present wife, Judy, was a rugged gal from San Francisco. She made it all the way to Mexico City. When he proposed marriage, she turned him down. They came back to New Orleans by bus.

Ricky was in love. He threatened to kill himself unless she married him. She said, "What the hell," and went ahead and married him. They had a host of friends. One was Marie, a cute little Italian girl who came into the studio around ten that evening. I could see that she was wasn't Ricky's style. She wasn't tall and blonde, and she had brown eyes, but she took a shine to me. Ricky and Judy bugged out and we faced the consequences together.

The way I looked at it and her, this very possibly could be the last woman that would come my way on this mortal

plane. I approached the repast with a kind of religious fervor.

The solemnities continued throughout the night. Marie didn't know what the special excitement was all about, but she reveled in it. At last, as the first light of day showed in the great studio window, I surrendered to sleep.

It was morning in New Orleans. The sun came up red, throwing a warm shaft of light through the tall window of the studio. Ricky was in a corner near the window, bathed in it. He was hacking away at that pristine block of limestone. I nudged Marie and we stumbled out of the hideaway bed. Judy was out in the tiny kitchen. I could smell the aroma of coffee.

I sat on the edge of the bed and stared at Ricky. He was obviously an optimist or else he didn't understand what he was in for. I wondered whether he expected to get back alive and finish that crouching nude.

"Hey Captain," he said, "They found out where you are.

They called this morning. Some gal from the radio station who has a program called "New Orleans Honored Guest" wants to see you. How does it feel to be New Orleans honored guest?"

"Lousy," I said. I got up and stretched. My bones creaked. I leaned over and kissed Marie.

I had a cup of coffee and climbed down the rickety outside staircase and wobbled over to the radio station. The interviewer had blonde hair, blue eyes, and a couple of knockers that jumped up at you. She was tall and curved and even statuesque. I was about to ask her if she would like to take a canter down to Mexico City with me. "We go on the air in fifteen minutes," she said.

The engineer in the glass booth raised his arm and we were on the air. After I was introduced I talked a blue streak for fifteen minutes. I didn't let her get a word in edgeways. I remembered back when George Hicks asked me over a nationwide hookup whether I considered myself a hero. I know all about the tricks that interviewers play on you. I ran this one right off the air.

She looked at me petulantly after the light went out and the broadcast was over. I said, "I wonder what it would be like to kiss you?"

"Why don't you try?"

It wasn't half bad. I made a date with her for that night and took off for the Port of Embarkation.

The ST250 was in a turmoil. They were installing a two-way radio in the pilothouse. They were stowing provisions in the lazarette. There were workmen climbing all over her. I had papers to sign and receipts to initial and charts to lug back from the Navy office. Virgilio was on board wandering around. I gave him a copy of *Leaves of Grass* so that he would keep out of the road and read. I figured that he would dig Walt Whitman.

The vessel was in a crescendo of activity, when suddenly Virgilio appeared in the wheelhouse. He came at me with the book in his hand and his eyes bulging. "You air," he breathed. I backed away. He pursued me. "You air," he breathed in my face, "You air that serves me with the breath to speak."

He dug Walt Whitman.

We cast off her lines and went down river to get her bunkers filled. The chief engineer was a sawed-off guy with a bristling head of hair. His name was Peacock. He was brought up in Chicago, and he swaggered around like a gangster. On the way back from the oil depot I rang the telegraph to cut the engine and made a sailboat landing at the dock.

Peacock was up in arms. He evidently wanted me to come tearing in full throttle and ring "Full Astern" just before impact. In his book that would have been a vote of confidence. It never occurred to the guy that this was my first command and that I hardly knew him. It would have been a fine time to collide with a dock in plain sight of the shipping director.

I made the vessel secure and rode uptown to have dinner with Ricky, Judy, and the gal from the radio station. We had a grand feast at Antoine's and we got all gassed up. The radio gal was a sharp cookie, Ricky and Judy were in rare form, and I found myself at last all alone with her naked beside me.

I stared at that expanse of white flesh with the moonlight sweeping across it. She was truly beautiful and young and luscious. In the kaleidoscopic apprehension of that time I saw in this girl the woman I wanted to marry. If I could only check my bet, hold her for some distant time.

What distant time did I have? Could I ask her to share with me a vague and uncertain future? What were my chances of survival? I saw myself like the vessel I commanded, snagged on a reef and breaking up in a violent surf. My head spun like a top-heavy tug going over before the onslaught of a massive wave. I had wasted by life substance in a panic of fear the night before.

I struggled to my feet and stared down at her. She had

come to me one night too late. How could I explain what had happened to me? You win some and you lose some. I knew then that this was the big one I lost. There wasn't a damn thing I could do about it. I felt like an impotent old fart.

She got dressed and I took her home. When I kissed her goodnight, I felt crushed, broken, robbed. It was a mournful walk back down Bourbon Street to Ricky's place. I felt doomed and vaguely resentful. I wondered how in hell I was going to survive the long night that lay before me and the ocean.

I walked into a bar on the corner of Royal and Bourbon for a bracer. Old Fats was still playing the piano. He asked me what I would like to hear.

"Do you know "Fit As A Fiddle and Ready for Love?" I tossed a buck in the basket.

"Yeah man."

"Well, goddamn it, play it."

10

Surprisingly, the sun came up in the morning just as if nothing was happening. I went down to the Port of Embarkation and went aboard my new command.

The previous captain of the ST250 was there picking up his luggage. He had no license either, but he sported an omelet on the visor of his cap and four gold stripes on his sleeve. My uniform was a grey civilian suit. I was proud of it. It was what all the old-time skippers wore. It was the badge of a Merchant Marine officer. We were civilians who went to sea come hell or high water.

When you came right down to it, drowning in a civilian suit was no worse than going under dressed like a rear admiral. We would all be together at last in Fiddler Green. They were going there by the hundreds. Five thousand men went down choking and bubbling to their deaths during the first few months of the war. It damn near wiped out the profession. That's why I was taking the ST250 out to Honolulu without a license.

There were endless delays in the departure. It was just as if Major Ecols, who directed the operation, was looking at the casualty lists and hated to see them go. His father owned a string of tugs and he loved them. He had grown up on them.

I spent some time in the galley drinking coffee and getting acquainted with the crew. I got to know Eddie Reineke, the first mate who was like my right arm all the way out to the Pacific. The messman was a heavy-set fellow by the name of Kidd, B. L. K. Kidd. His parents had a sense of humor. So did Kidd. He was laughing all the time.

Kidd wanted to get out of the galley. He took the job because it was the only one on a tug going out. When he found that it was going out across the Pacific, he smiled and took it in his stride. None of us knew until I pulled him out of the Mississippi one night months later, after he had gone down three times, that he didn't know how to swim.

I went over to Higgins and I had Kidd transferred to the deck department. He went out as an able-bodied seaman. We shipped another messman. His name was Namb. The crew called him "Numb." He was born in Milwaukee, and he talked as if he had just come off the pickle boat. His parents were German, and they still conversed in the mother tongue.

Namb was too inflexible to adopt the everyday American dialect from school or from the gutter. He was doing his laundry that morning, and he asked me if it would be all right if he hung his drawers on the signal halyards to dry.

I explained to him gently that it might be misunderstood for a distress signal. Then he asked me if we were going to go out in deep water.

"Not much deeper than your bathtub at home." I decided to have a little chat with the boy. I invited him up to my quarters. The crew was a rough gang, and I knew that they would turn this guy's life into a living hell. I wanted to prepare him for what surely lay ahead.

After I closed the door of the cabin I said, "Look Namb, this gang we have on board is a heartless lot. I am going to give you some fatherly advice. I was a young fellow going to sea, and I had to learn to put up with a lot of horse play. Let me tell you something, you have to learn to keep your mouth shut. You will learn more by listening than by asking foolish questions. If you keep your mouth shut they will figure you for an old-time sailor, and they will leave you alone. If you want to know anything, come up and ask me.

It was like asking the poor bastard to stop breathing. He peered at me through his horn-rimmed glasses. "By the way," I went on, "it wasn't right for me to kid you. We will be going out into deep water. Try and remember that you can drown just as easily in your bathtub."

He nodded violently and bowed out. I knew that he was in for a hard time.

It was in the early part of 1944. In the years that ensued, fifty million parents had no more luck than I did trying to give their young people advice.

And who in hell were we to give advice?

In those fateful years you didn't need advice. What you needed was luck. Months after I sat for my ticket, I was approached by a middle-aged second engineer from the corn belt. He had been to sea for several months. "Captain," he said, "I would like to have a few words with you privately. I need some advice."

We walked into the chart room. "What can I do for you?"

"It is kind of personal," he said, "I would like to know whether I should be faithful to my wife?"

I knew that chaplains as well as any kind of morale-building programs were nonexistant in the Merchant Marine. I felt sorry for this guy and I knew what his problem was, but I decided to have some fun with him anyway.

"Hmm," I said, with the most patriarchal expression I could put on, "we will have to look that one up."

I pulled down from the rack the voluminous edition of the *American Practical Navigator* by Nathaniel Bowditch. Thumbing through the pages, I volunteered that his question would most likely be entered under "storms."

"Now, it says here that if you are approaching the vicinity

of a hurricane, you should exercise caution. Do you exercise caution, Brown?"

"Oh yes."

"Good. It also says that in the northern hemisphere . . . we are in the northern hemisphere, you know."

"Oh yes, I know."

"Well, in the northern hemisphere it is wise to turn and run with the wind on your port quarter. Do you understand that, Mr. Brown?"

"Oh yes," he said, "but what about my wife?"

Standing before him, I looked at him solemnly over the massive volume. "Well, I should say that your wife should do the same thing. Turn and run with the wind on her port quarter. Your wife is in the northern hemisphere, is she not?"

"Oh yes," he said.

"In that case you had better get in touch with her as soon as we hit port and advise her accordingly."

He nodded like Namb and left the chart room like a man redeemed. The sea, however, knows no favorites. Brown was lost on a freighter that was torpedoed off North Africa. Sometimes I wonder if his old lady is still running around the northern hemisphere with the wind on her port quarter.

11

Several months before I became a captain, I had sailed down to Panama on a sixty-foot transport vessel under the sporadic command of a seasick young skipper by the name of Lawrence.

Upon arrival in Panama we had been quartered temporarily in an Army compound, awaiting a ship to take us back to New Orleans by way of San Francisco.

Among the permanent inhabitants of that establishment was a tugboat captain who had run afoul of Army regulations and the law. He had deliberately run his tug aground and capsized her. His name was Dyer, and he came from a small town in Texas. The curious thing about him was the enormous fondness he had for the Mexican people.

I talked with him for a long time. I found out that he was beholden to the son of a wetback who had managed to get into a medical school. Dyer's wife was critically ill, and this young doctor, answering an emergency, pulled her through.

It was a touching story. I never found out whether Dyer's sympathy embraced other minorities. I figured that he had a good heart. His difficulties sprang from the fact that the Army would not grant him leave to go home and visit his wife. He had been down in that evil climate for three solid years. In a fit of frustration he wrecked the vessel he commanded. He was under house arrest, awaiting trial.

Dyer asked me if I would deliver two letters for him, take them to the States, and mail them. One was to his wife in Texas, and the other one was to a colonel at the Port of Embarkation in New Orleans. I felt sorry for him and I agreed to do it. It was tricky.

We came back to the States by way of San Francisco. When I passed through customs, one of the guards said, "Do you have any letters in that bag?"

Evidently, information about our operations in the Pacific was leaking back to the Japanese through letters brought into our country by servicemen returning from the Pacific War Zone.

I hesitated, and then I said, "No."

The officer looked at me dubiously. Then he said, "It will go hard with you son if you are not telling the truth."

"No," I said, "No letters."

He let me go through. There was no information in those letters that would have done the enemy a damn bit of good, but I felt like an international spy.

We boarded a train bound for New Orleans. It was a Pullman. I lit the night light over the berth and took out the letters and memorized them. When I was sure that I knew them by heart, I opened the train window a crack. As the train sped along the tracks, every five minutes I tore off a tiny fragment of one of the letters and threw it out the window. It took hours to get rid of those letters. Instead of hanging me, all they could do now is arrest me for littering.

In the morning I wrote a letter to his wife with the gist of his letter to her. When I got back to the Port of Embarkation, I went in to see the colonel and delivered the message orally.

Dyer went through a court-martial, was acquitted and released. He returned to New Orleans. Either the influence of his friend the colonel or the well-known propensity of those tugs to capsize on their own swung the tide in his favor. Nonetheless, I wondered whether anybody would have done as much for me as I did for Dyer.

When the time arrived to go down to the Navy office and get my sailing orders, I was informed that another tug would be sailing out with the ST250, bound for Honolulu. We were directed to sail in consort. The name of the other tug was ST249. The name of the captain was Dyer.

It was the same guy. I met him at the Navy office. He was very stiff, very formal. I mentioned the letters I had delivered for him. He stared at me sternly and drew a blank.

There were a couple of loose ends to take care of before we could shove off. One was that Navy-type anchor that was lashed to the deck on the forepeak. I had known for years that a stockless anchor like that was absolutely useless on a coral bottom. I had tried to get them to swap it for a kedge anchor with no success.

Eddie Reineke, with patriotic zeal mixed with a touch of larceny, came to the rescue. Waiting for the lunch break while the workmen were over at the canteen, Eddie appropriated a fork lift that was standing unattended, picked up that Navy anchor, and ran up the ramp into the storage shed. The supply sergeant was out to lunch too. Eddie dumped the Navy anchor, picked up the five-hundred-pound kedge anchor, and brought it back aboard.

The mystery about a kedge anchor that was transformed into a Navy anchor is a metamorphosis that bugged a certain supply sergeant for months. If it is any compensation for all the hell he caught, one night in a howling storm on a lee coast that kedge jammed one of its pointed flukes into a crevice in a coral reef and saved ten lives.

The other matter was the meat that the commissary had furnished us. It was described by W. D. the cook as "carcass."

After we shoved off, we pulled in briefly at a public dock at the Industrial Canal. Waiting for us there was two hundred pounds of porterhouse and sirloin steaks.

I had an official order that directed all suppliers to furnish under penalty of fine and imprisonment any supplies of food or fuel that the vessel required.

I had ordered the steaks from the fanciest caterer in New Orleans. I signed the receipt and we turned down stream to follow the ST249.

This voyage, for all its jeopardy, was bound to be a catered affair. If we had to go down we were going to go down feeling good. Despite all the apprehension, the euphoria that attends every departure prevailed even through the steady drizzle that created a soft haze along the banks of the Mississippi.

12

The ST250 ducked into a canal that led to the locks. The gates swung closed behind us, and we sank to the level of Lake Borgne. The ST249 had already passed through. When we reached the drawbridge our companion vessel was nowhere in sight. The drawbridge along the railroad trestle was closed, and an interminable string of freight cars was rumbling across our path. I rang the telegraph to stop the engine, and we drifted in the fog.

Eddie Reineke, who had been at the wheel, lit a cigarette and stood beside me at the pilothouse window as I stared out into the wet gloom. "Captain," he said, "I don't want to sound nosy but where did all those cigarettes come from? I counted four cases of cigarettes under your bunk."

"Eddie," I said without turning around, "do you know what J. P. Morgan said when he heard that General Sherman described war as hell?"

"What did he say?"

"He said, 'Yeah, but there's a buck in it.' "

Eddie looked baffled.

"Yesterday I went over to the Army commissary. I wanted

to buy a few cartons of cigarettes for the crew, four different brands. Do you know what they told me?"

"What did they tell you?"

"They said that I would have to buy a case of each brand. I bought four cases. There are fifty cartons in a case. I paid a nickle a pack."

Eddie smiled. You never had to spell it out for Eddie. He had been to Central America, and he knew that you could get a dollar a pack for them down there.

"It doesn't pay to argue with the Army, Eddie."

The drawbridge opened as the red caboose trailed away, and we followed the channel markers through the Mississippi Sound. Turning at Grand Pass, we entered Mobile Bay late in the day.

It was all safe and easy going. As much as the tug rolled, there wasn't a wave big enough to worry about while out around the Delta of the Mississippi, which we had by-passed while the submarines were lying in wait. I had heard that they were knocking off ships like clay pigeons in a shooting gallery.

"Eddie, what do you think the chances are of catching a torpedo?"

"Not a chance," said Eddie, "A sub commander would have to be nuts to carry a torpedo all the way across the Atlantic to waste it on a tug."

"How about a five-inch fragmentary shell?"

"Yeah, they could throw one of those at us."

"I doubt it, Eddie. He would be crazy to reveal his position for so small a prize."

The weather was our enemy. In the Intercoastal Waterway it was no problem. That's where these tugs were designed to run. There was a moderate wind out of the northeast when we changed course at the whistle buoy, passed the old tower and the abandoned lighthouse, and headed out across the Gulf of Mexico for Tampa.

The watches were set. I took the 8 to 12 watch, which is the conventional captain's watch, Virgilio Varga was on the 12 to 4 watch, and Eddie Reineke was the officer on watch from 4 to 8. There are generally three mates sharing the three watches so that the old man who is always on call can get some sleep.

I had to carry the burden of my own watch and still be available if there was an emergency or a problem on any of the other watches. When I told Captain Lord that it was no picnic, he knew what I was talking about.

The compass course from the sea buoy off Mobile Bay to the sea buoy off Egmont Channel that led into St. Pete and Tampa was 110. That course suited me right down to the ground. Any number with 11 in it was a lucky number for me.

The chart table was right behind the wheel in the pilothouse. The chart of the Gulf of Mexico was spread out on it. A tiny flashlight that did not compete with the faint light of the compass binnacle illuminated the eastern section of the chart. The parallel ruler lay along our course, its partner reaching up to bisect the compass rose. It fell squarely at 110 and I felt good about it. While I stared at it, my mind drifted back to my early years, when I took violent issue with a sweet old biddy called Aunt Ella. Aunt Ella was a numerology nut.

"Eight," she declared, "is a successful number." I tried to smile indulgently. "And eleven is an even more successful number."

Despite all my cynicism it occurred to me that I could find a course that added up to 8 or 11 all around the compass rose. Starting with 8 and progressively 17 and 26 and 35 and 44, I could go full circle with every course right up to 350, adding up to the magic number of 8. Furthermore, if I wished to modify the course slightly, I could resort to 353, which added up to 11.

In all those frenetic and violent years I never set a course that didn't add up to 8 or 11. The practice had certain definite advantages. If I came on watch and asked the man at the helm what course he was steering and it didn't add up to 8 or 11, I knew he was off course.

Like most superstitions that one is secretly ashamed of, I never let on why I set such zany courses. Pondering the wide variations in direction that this overhatted tug was subject to as it yawed widely underway, it seemed foolish to ignore a notion that made me feel better. Considering the variety of personalities in the ten men who made up the crew and that all our lives hinged on the element of chance, it appeared to be sheer folly to ignore anything that seemed to bring good luck. Certainly one could hardly hope to escape the verdict of one's chromosomes, or attempt to duck the destiny of one's genes.

As for myself, I had inherited, along with some qualities I may have reason to be proud of, an unfortunate physical handicap from my maternal grandfather.

Grandpa was a giant of a man. When he was eighty I wouldn't have dared swap wallops with him. He was a math genius and a master builder; a man of fantastic ability, perseverance and taste. Nothing seemed beyond his capabilities. He also had a hernia.

The form in which that weakness was transmitted down two generations to me was what is known clinically as an enlarged inguinal ring. Grandpa had his sewn up a couple of times, but in the arduous and vehement exercise of his great physical stamina, he broke it open both times.

He gave up on surgical procedure and acquired a truss. I can still remember it hanging on the back of a chair while Grandpa was bending over a plan for a million-dollar complex that he was drawing.

After the sketch was completed, grandpa would harness himself up with that truss and go out and contract for the excavation and the masonry and then take charge of the whole operation. He was a self-taught architect, planner, builder. I worshipped the old man.

I had been turned down in the early days of the war in a

bid for a commission in the Navy because I had an enlarged inguinal ring. They weren't so fussy in the Merchant Marine. They were so desperate for sailors that they would have taken me with a glass eye and a wooden leg.

As I climbed the windward ladder that evening after dinner as the ST250 was nodding her way across the Gulf of Mexico, the vessel gave a violent lurch. I felt something go. I knew then that I was in the same boat as grandpa. I had a right inguinal hernia.

The Navy had its reasons for being reluctant to grant me a commission. A hernia can be its own kind of time bomb. It can close up on part of your gut, and in that strangulation cause a condition known as peritonitis, which can kill you in a matter of hours. Nonetheless, I was not about to run to a doctor who might have reported the condition and put an end to my new command.

We sighted the light at Egmont Key in the early hours of the morning. We made the passage up through the channel in a downpour and chugged up toward Tampa. That morning, on the way to the Navy office to pick up my sailing orders for the next leg of the voyage down to Havana, I stopped at a surgical supply house. I had no prescription from a doctor. I had cash. You could buy anything you wanted in Tampa for cash. That's where Lawson bought his license. I slapped down twenty dollars and bought myself a brand new, shiny, right-handed truss.

13

The naval officer who made out the sailing orders for the ST250 in Tampa was a country boy from Alabama. He said, "Do you want to swing around Key West and head for Yucatan, or would you rather go through the backdoor into Key West and tie up for the night? You can proceed to Havana the next morning.

I said, "I'll take Havana."

"Good idea," he said, "You can get your horn scraped in Havana. You will receive further sailing orders from the port captain in Key West."

We took our departure from the whistle buoy at Egmont Key at eight o'clock in the morning. The sky cleared and the wind was out of the east providing a smooth sea. We ran past Gasparilla Island and close aboard Sanibel. We could see the tourists hunting shells on Sanibel, just as if there was no war going on at all.

Toward dark we ducked into shallow water in San Carlos Bay and dropped the hook, with the palm trees to windward and the 16-mile light flashing twice at the southern end of Sanibel.

Our sailing instructions specified that at night we were to take refuge in port or in shoal water to avoid the possibility of being mistaken for a submarine and then being bombed by our coastal patrol planes. I had no idea where in hell I was supposed to find shallow water in the run between California and Honolulu. Maybe that was what was bugging Namb.

The rest of the crew was only too happy to let me do the worrying. There were a lot of bridges to cross, and I took heart in the apparent cheerfulness of the crew. I hesitated to contaminate that cheerfulness with my fears.

Ricky came up on the boat deck after dinner and we shot the bull. He told me about his part in a revolution in Mexico. He was pinned down in a foxhole for a night and a day, and he whiled away the hours studying the progress of a battle between two colonies of ants while the bullets screamed an inch or two above his head.

"It was a hell of a war. A lot of ants died," Ricky laughed. "I forgot all about the revolution. I identified with the black ants. When they wiped out the red ants I knew I was going to be O.K."

I didn't confide my fears to Ricky. Being a skipper was a lonely business. There were nine lives to worry about besides my own. I hit the sack. It was not easy to get to sleep. The little ship rocked gently in the tide, and the stars moved slowly across the sky.

In the morning we took off, with the wind out of the north adding an extra knot to the speed of the tug.

Our course was 170. Late that afternoon we picked up the beacon off Cape Sable and followed the buoys into Key West.

Key West was blacked out. I walked through the dark streets. It was a moonlit night and the old gingerbread houses were ghostly in the soft light. I remembered the day more than a year before when I had given Captain Erbe that painting of a tugboat struggling to make port off Sand Key. I wondered whether he had survived the frightful jeopardy of these top-heavy tugs. There was no way of telling. The Army people were ominously close-mouthed about the casualties and the capsizings.

I went back aboard the ST250 and had a cup of coffee. About twelve o'clock Eddie came aboard. He had a black eye and a bloody nose; his hands were all cut and bleeding; and he was drunk as a coot. We dragged him into his bunk and he flaked out.

I cornered Eddie before breakfast. "What in hell happened to you last night?"

"I had a few beers and I went aboard the ST249, which came into Key West last night after we did. I thought that it was the ST250, and I asked the crew what the hell they were doing aboard our vessel. They claimed that it was their tugboat. I called them a bunch of damn liars, and I began to throw them out."

"Then the fight started," I said.

"Yeah, I threw most of them out, but they kept coming back in. It was a hell of a row."

I looked at Eddie's eye. It was black and swollen and his nose was all puffed up. "You don't want to go back and settle things over at the ST249 do you? I'll go along with you in case you have to continue the war."

"No," said Eddie, "It was my mistake. Those guys are O.K. I'll go over alone and settle it."

I hung around until Eddie came back from the ST249. I asked him how it went.

"A bunch of them were pretty beat up. I said that I was sorry. They laughed and we shook hands."

I took off for the Navy office. There were crowds of sailors in the street. Key West was a Navy town. The Navy officer gave me our sailing orders clear down to Panama. He said, "We are expecting a heavy northeaster today. The Gulf Stream gets rough when the wind and the current collide." He shook my hand and wished me well.

Peacock had the engine going when I got back to the tug. We took in the lines and stood out through the channel to the light at Sand Key and headed for Havana. I thought about Captain Erbe again as we ran out and I wondered whether the ST250 was as tender as the vessel we brought into Key West. Our course was 242 to compensate for the ferocious current of the Gulf Stream. About a mile out it began to kick up. Peacock had brains enough to bolt the engine room doors as the vessel began to rock and take seas aboard the main deck. I told Eddie to go down and make sure that the doors of all the cabins were dogged.

He came back up and said, "It doesn't make a hell of a lot of difference. The water shloshes into the cabins even with the doors jammed closed."

The wind was on our port quarter and the tug, taking advantage of the assist, moved into the leaden seas. It was overcast and there was little of that well-known Gulf Stream blue. It was an evil winter sea, and the whitecaps raced along with us as we struggled to make a landfall before it rolled us over.

We had ninety miles to go. With a fair wind the ST250 could do eleven knots. We were bucking the Gulf Stream, which cost us at least four of those. At best, we could not hope to make port before nine o'clock.

Around ten in the morning the seas began to grow in size, and they became sharper as we approached the center of the current. The vessel plunged her short forefoot into the cavernous depths and rocked back like a hobby-horse. Then she rolled and lifted again for another gigantic splash.

The deck gang were all up in the pilothouse now. The cook had abandoned the galley and some of the crew were crawling down the fidley skylight to warm up below.

The Gulf Stream was the acid test of the vessel's ability to live in violent and turbulent water. We had the advantage of a fair wind and the tug seemed to sense the possibility of making it into port. If the wind had swung around to the east in a direct confrontation with the current, we would have capsized. The crazy little tug kept slugging away.

It was a long day. I didn't ever want another one like it. I knew damn well that there would be more. It was comforting to hear that Enterprise diesel clicking away. I began to believe that Peacock, who had been employed in Chicago as a mechanic on these engines, was really my ace in the hole. If the engine quit now we were goners.

How reliable the chief engineer was remained a question. There are politics aboard any vessel when there are more than two people in the crew. There are black-gang politics and there are deck-monkey politics. My pipeline to engine room politics was my friend Ricky. Ricky was no blabbermouth, but I gathered that all was not sweetness and light down below. In fact, the engine room seethed with resentment.

Tex, the first assistant engineer, was a surly product of the Panhandle. The second assistant engineer was that soulful cornfed guy from the Middle West, who wanted to know whether to be faithful to his wife. The only people I could count on in a pinch were Ricky the oiler, Eddie the mate, and Kidd the deckhand. All the rest were imponderables. The most imponderable of all was Peacock.

This bandy-legged product of the Chicago slums was one hell of an engineer. He was also a vicious drunk, a braggart and the ultimate example of antisocial behavior. When he was of a mind, he had a kind of ingratiating charm. Outside of his domain in the engine room, where his dominance was a source of security, I didn't trust him as far as I could kick a pie.

A few miles astern of us our companion vessel was pounding away. If we needed an objective view of the kind of hell we were going through, all we had to do was to look at what was happening to the ST249. She rose and pitched and wallowed in the treacherous seas as madly as we did.

There was something insane about the business of sending

94

vessels out as poorly equipped to handle heavy weather as these. But then there is nothing sane about war. War is a maniac, urging the man in charge to do something, anything. The courage to do nothing, when nothing is the thing to do, has never earned a decoration. A smart marine operator would have rebuilt these vessels, kept them in port, or sent them out as deck cargos on Liberty ships.

There were no decorations being handed out to anyone in the Merchant Marine. There was simply the inescapable reality of the War Manpower Act, which read, "Go to sea or be drafted."

A sailor by profession preferred to go to sea.

This particular sea was unmitigated agony, but every man aboard would have chosen it over having to take a lot of shit from a top sergeant.

It was impossible to picture a guy like Peacock in an organized army. He was that kind of violent character you read about in the hairy stories of the lawless West. He was cagey too.

Peacock knew that I didn't have a license, and for that matter, neither did he. Sometimes he would climb up out of the engine room and stare around. Every landfall we made, every lighthouse that lifted above the horizon added to his conviction that I knew my business. But all the lighthouses and all the sea buoys that we hit on the nose never sufficed to prove to him that I could find my way across twenty-four hundred miles of the Pacific to Honolulu.

As for myself, I trusted that Lew Higgins had put a capable guy in the engine room. What that guy did when he wasn't in the engine room was none of my business.

As for my method of navigation, it was the same as the navigation used by the Conquistadors. It was the navigation practiced by Balboa and Cortez and Columbus. It consisted of the three L's: log, lead, and latitude. The Army had failed to provide us with a chronometer, without which an accurate longitude is impossible. We did have what is known as a hack watch on board—on the long chance that we could intercept a time tick from some nearby vessel. But the latitude by noon sight, soundings, and reading of the log were the only clue to our position.

No licensed officer in his right mind would have shoved off as badly equipped as we were. A year or so later, after I had received my mate's ticket for any tonnage and any ocean, I was provided with a chronometer and the proper tables. I shuddered to think of the chance I took on that impossible tugboat.

To figure a longitude from an observation of a celestial body in that squirrel cage of a pilothouse, one would have to be a miracle worker. The wind piped up to forty and fifty miles an hour. The boat dug its stubby nose into green water and wallowed with a load of it. It must have been awful down below.

Ricky climbed up through the fidley and tried to tell me what it was like down there. It was hard to be empathetic while spinning the wheel to counter every erratic smashing sea. I didn't dare trust anyone else with the helm.

It went on for hours. It grew dark, and now the terror of night compounded the ominous thrust of the violent sea. It seemed almost a godsend when the light on Morro Castle beckoned us into the sanctuary of the Havana Harbor channel.

The last storm you fight your way through is always the worst, but this one was a likely candidate for the most terrifying one of all.

We picked up a pilot at the sea buoy and ran along the lights of the Malecon into the stillness of the Havana Harbor. We tied up to a pier. I lit a cigarette and faced the wonder and the romance of old Havana from the pilothouse window.

W. D. brewed some coffee and started to heat up some food. The men opened the doors of their cabins and found that the salt water mixed with the oil that clung to the deck had soaked and filthied up every stitch of clothes they owned. They ate and went ashore with whatever they had on their backs. We decided to worry about the mess in their cabins in the morning.

14

Havana blossomed in the early sunlight. The necklace of ancient buildings along the waterfront sparkled. There was an allover pattern of whitecaps, in the harbor, and Morro Castle on the point loomed grey and foreboding against the sky. Some of the crew were still asleep after the anxiety of the passage, and the rest were still shacked up somewhere in the city. W. D. fixed me an omelet and I took off along the Malecon and walked north along the harbor's edge. I found a decrepit old bumboat tied up along the concrete wharf and paid the skipper of the craft a quarter to row me out to Morro Castle. I had to get away from the tug. I needed a breather.

Looking down from the hoary ramparts across the old town, I thought about the part that Havana played in the boisterous history of the New World. I could see the tall square-rigged ships of war raking each other with cannon shot in the battle of the great European powers to control that strategic port. I could imagine pirate ships with their raked masts and ponderous merchantmen lying side by side in a fragile truce, sweating out the greater jeopardy of a hurricane that raged in the violent stream outside the breakwater.

Over the horizon, beyond that endless edge of royal blue, a gigantic continent writhed in what seemed at times like a losing war.

Havana was neutral. The average *hombre* on the streets knew less than nothing about the issues of the war and couldn't care less. The thing that bothered him was the scarcity of tourist loot. Havana was gripped in a catastrophic depression. War had tossed a monkey wrench into the gearbox. The machinery of entertainment was at a standstill. You could buy a shot of rum for less than you had to pay for a bottle of coke. The bars were jammed with girls looking for a buck. They were girls who might otherwise have stayed married or eked out a living back in their home towns. The economic condition of the country drove them into Havana, where they crowded the bars and the brothels in fierce competition for the American dollar.

War had brought its own kind of crisis to Havana. I began to see what the naval officer in Tampa was talking about. The price was two bucks. You could even get a girl for a dollar or for fifty cents. When I ran out of cash, I got a redheaded beauty for nothing. She was a dreamy piece if you could overlook that missing front tooth.

I came back from Morro Castle, finished my business with the Navy office, and went into town. I wandered about, remembering other times and other ships. I stopped and had a beer with Marta, the fat madam who had propositioned Captain Larry.

Marta said, "How is it with my friend Larry the captain?"

"Baby," I said, "I wish I knew."

"What are you doing now?" she said.

"I am captain of a tugboat."

"Now you are captain. That is better. Captain Larry was no captain."

"I guess they found that out."

"But where is your uniform?" She rolled her tremendous weight toward me and looked me up and down. "What are you doing in a business suit?"

"A lot of captains wear business suits."

"Yes," she said, "but now it is war." She shook her head sadly. "If they catch you they will shoot you as a spy."

I looked at the fat old biddy. She was telling the truth. Why hadn't somebody brought that up before? Why did it have to come from a whorehouse madam in Havana?

"I'll be damned," I said. "Maybe one day I will buy a uniform. Maybe after I get my license."

I sat there drinking my beer and wondering if I would ever make it back to sit for my mate's ticket and to buy a uniform.

I said goodbye to the madam and left the place. Down the avenue I found Ricky in a bookstall thumbing through some books printed in Spanish. I waited until he was finished browsing and we took off down the avenue. The girls, recognizing his Mexican accent, crowded around him. The Cubans were vastly in awe of Mexicans, just as we are impressed with the British. Ricky could have had any one of these girls, or all of them, but he was being faithful to Judy, the statuesque wife who had made it with him to Mexico City.

I could sense that I embarrassed Ricky by attempting to converse in Spanish with the girls who tagged after him. He acted just as I probably acted as a kid when my grandmother, who sounded as if she had just come off the pickle boat, tried out her English in the presence of my friends.

After being hushed-up a few times, I decided that I would never be able to practice my Spanish in his company, and I cut out on my own.

I had a couple more beers in Sloppy Louie's and wound up in a homey little whorehouse on a side street. The pompous madam gave me a cup of coffee and paraded her wares. She had two girls. One was a sweet little brown thing who had just come in from the Batabatan and the other was a wretched looking, painted English hag who had fallen on evil days in Havana.

My curiosity was engaged by the painted English lady, but the revulsion I felt was above and beyond the call of duty. I paid the madam her fee and went upstairs with the little brown thing. Her name was Lily. Lily was positively overjoyed at being chosen. It was hard to understand. It didn't seem possible that anyone could have chosen that English hag. But then there were men in Havana who somewhere, somehow must have relished that pretense of aristocracy in her manner. There must be an accounting for taste.

Lily, however, was lovely. She was as joyous as a newlywed. She told me about her home, her childhood, and the wayward guy she married and who had left her with a child. The baby was at home with her mother. There was no room for bitterness in Lily. She was totally responsive. We lay together in the bed in that little room, with the light of a neon sign blinking off and on in the window, and I thought about all the stories I had heard about cold and grasping prostitutes who were perfunctory and calloused. Maybe I was lucky, but it seemed like every one I knew were women who were making the best of a cruel and heartless situation.

Money makes the difference. These girls had come from destitute families. Invariably, there was someone for whom they were doing it, a child, a mother, an ailing relative. While they were at it they did it for their own pleasure as well. They were not fools.

I recalled the father of a friend of mine when I was going to school. He told his son to "Pay for it like a man. Don't scratch for it like a dog."

I paid for it like a man, and I threw in the rest of the money that I had in my wallet. It was worth it.

I ran into some of the crew off the ST249 who had made it into Havana Harbor. I asked them how Dyer was doing and they shrugged. They went into a bar and I kept on walking.

Wandering down toward the harbor, I came to a park and sat on a bench under the trees. There was a bright-eyed young Cuban fellow sitting next to me.

"May I speak with you in English," he began.

"You will have to speak with me in English. I don't know enough Spanish to order a tortillo."

"I am practicing to speak English."

"Fire away." I said.

"What does that mean, 'fire away'?"

I held up my hand, pointed my finger like a gun, and said, "Bang, bang!"

"Si," he said and laughted. "Fire away." Then he added, "Why are they fighting all over the world?"

"Hitler is a bad man. We have to stop him."

"Then why do we not fight?"

"Maybe because you are a Spanish people, and in Spain Franco is not angry with Hitler."

"Si," he said, "They are both dictators. Sometimes I hear them talk in school of a dictator here in Cuba."

"The teachers talk of a dictator?"

"No, the students."

"Who knows," I said. If it remained bad as it was for the average Cuban, there was bound to be a dictator. That's when the redhead came along.

My young friend on the bench said, "Would you like to go to bed with her?"

"Sure," I said, "It is past my bedtime."

"I will ask her." He got up and spoke to the girl in Spanish. Then he brought her over and introduced her to me. He explained to her that I did not speak Spanish. "Do you like her?" he asked.

"I like her fine."

"She says that she likes you also."

"Tell her that I have no money."

"No dinero."

"De nada."

There followed a lengthy conversation between the student of English and the pretty streetwalker. At last he turned to me and said, "She would like to take you to the place where she lives, but her roommate is entertaining a rich man from the Oriente province." There was a pause during which the girl smiled at me. It didn't seem possible, but she acted coy, even reticent.

"She says that she would like to have you go with her to a hotel. She says that it doesn't matter that you have no money. She will pay."

I thanked my new friend, took the arm of the lovely redhead, and we went off together, just as if we had been going steady for years.

Her name was Stella. Her ignorance of English was absolute. She was altogether delightful, in all but that missing front tooth. It wasn't hard to get used to. That one flaw served to accentuate her other attributes. She had a perfect figure, a radiant complexion, and a magnificent sweep of auburn hair. She held my arm tightly, and we walked in silence along the deserted streets of Havana.

It was two o'clock in the morning when we stopped at a hotel along the ocean in the Vedado section of town. Stella spoke to the clerk and gave him some money. We walked up five flights, and Stella opened a door that overlooked the sea. We stood together for a long time, looking out over the dark expanse of water and at the stars. Then, because she was tired and I was tired, we went to sleep like two innocent children.

Near dawn, Stella stirred and moved close to me. I felt the sweetness of her, and I longed to kiss her, but she did not try, and I did not insist. It was enough that ultimately we came together, with only a diaphanous membrane between us that was all but lost to our consciousness in the thrust of our desire.

The sun burst through the picture window in the morning like a bombshell. With signs and signals like a deaf-mute,

Stella indicated that she was going down to bring me some coffee. I dressed and waited for her on the balcony.

She went all the way down five flights and climbed back up with two containers of coffee and a half a dozen jelly doughnuts. We had breakfast in a kind of penthouse garden of the hotel, which was part of that necklace of the time-encrusted jewels of Havana.

We smiled at each other, drinking coffee in the sunshine. Hers was an altogether lovely smile, even without that tooth. The war and the terror of the ST250 seemed a million miles away.

I wish I could have told her in her own tongue how much I thought of her. I held her hand. When I rose to go, I pressed her close to me and walked away without a word. I went down the long stairwell as if I were walking away from some impossible dream. The gang was waiting for me on the tug when I showed up.

They had a legitimate gripe. Their clothes were ruined by salt water and the ugly filth that came up off the deck of the ST250. I sent for a dry cleaner.

There was no mention in my paper-of-authorization to suppliers for the services of a dry cleaner. There was, however, a paragraph stating that I could have the linen laundered. When the man came, I sent out all those clothes and had them dry cleaned. I told the man to bring me back a bill that said, "sheets and towels," and I would sign it.

Late that afternoon the crew's clothes came back spotless. Kidd had a fedora that came back cleaned and blocked. The bill read, "Two hundred sheets and six hundred towels."

Failing in an effort to explain to the dry cleaner that the bill would look as if we had a bacchanalian orgy in Havana, I asked him simply to make the bill read, "One hundred towels and three hundred sheets."

He shrugged, changed the bill, and I signed it, wondering what they would make of it when it showed up at the Port of Embarkation in New Orleans.

Early the next morning, just as we were about to shove off, a dog materialized on the dock. It was a male dog of average size with an infinite variety of antecedents. He jumped aboard our vessel, and Ricky boosted him up on the boat deck.

He came up to me with his tail swinging like a metronome and squatted on his haunches, as if to say, "Here I am, sign me on."

"Buster," I said, "you don't know what you are asking for. But if there is nothing better for you in Havana, welcome aboard."

He got up on all fours and licked my hand. I have an affinity for dogs. I have often wondered if they love me because I love them or because maybe I smell like a hamburger.

I have walked up and petted ferocious junkyard dogs, fierce guard dogs and indiscriminately fondled strange mutts, just as if I had known them from puppyhood. The proprietors watch with bulging eyes and jaws hanging when I walk up and pat the protectors of all that junk. It is just as if I had already discussed the problem with the dog, and we had decided that all that junk was not worth making a fuss about.

The trainers of attack dogs are also astonished, which surprises me, knowing that I speak the language of dogs. I share the sentiments of James Stephens, the Irish poet who dismissed a contingent of reporters who had come to meet him on his arrival on the *Queen Mary.*

He said, "I have nothing to say to you, gentlemen. I have a message from the dogs of Ireland for the dogs of America, and I intend to deliver it in person."

Buster curled up at my feet just behind the wheel and I rang the telegraph "slow ahead."

We moved out along the Malecon. Morro Castle threw its long shadow across the channel, and we passed from shadow into sunlight. We dropped the pilot at the sea buoy and turned to the west.

The wind was fair out of the southeast, and we ran until late that afternoon in the lee of the land. We entered Bahia Honda and dropped the hook in the stillness of the harbor. I didn't bother to launch the lifeboat, even though I knew of a place where you could get a marvelous meal for thirteen cents.

W. D. prepared a sufficient supper of salad with avocados and T-bone steaks. The guys in the black gang played poker in the galley half the night, and I found Virgilio walking around the boat deck mooning. He stopped me and said, "I can not go forward. How can I go forward when my heart is in New Orleans?"

"Forget it," I said. "All of us have left part of our lives behind us. You'll get used to it."

Varga shook his head. "How can I go forward? I cannot go forward when my heart is in New Orleans."

That is when it started. It was a refrain that persisted all the way around to California. It wasn't long before the crew took up the chant. You could catch snatches of it down below in the engine room. You could hear it in the pilot-house and in the galley. It became a universal lament. "How can I go forward? I cannot go forward when my heart is in New Orleans."

In the morning, we went forward nonetheless. We stood out to sea before dawn, and we ran the treacherous northwest coast of Cuba, whose outlying rocky islands are known as the Archipielago de los Colorados. Using the towering mountain peaks as ranges, by triangulation I could keep constant our distance off shore.

We passed a Cuban fishing sloop headed east. The fisherman was using his intimate knowledge of that complicated coastline to weave his way among the islands and the rocks. The vessel was gaff-rigged like my *Princess* and it had the same bowsprit, the same sheer, the same grace as my down east sloop.

The fisherman had a lure strung out behind him, and just as we came abeam, a barracuda grabbed it. We watched in quickly diminishing perspective as the fisherman fought to boat the fish; and before long all I had was a gnawing nostalgia for peacetime and my own vessel. Soon, the struggle to capture the frantic fish was nothing more than a blur on the horizon.

Following the example set by this fisherman, we ran as close as we dared to this dangerous shore, which spared us from having to breast the brutal assault of the current.

The lighthouse at Cabo San Antonio was sighted just after sundown; and we ran part of the way back into Ensenada de Corrientes to get out of the current that swung past the cape. The east wind had shifted to the northeast. I tried to find an anchorage that would avoid making a night at anchor as bad as the constant roll of the vessel by day.

We found it in the lee of the light at Cabo San Antonio. I took a bearing on a steady light ashore that gave us a fix in the event that she dragged her hook. The boys were bushed by the long run, and we sacked out early.

In the morning, there was the ST249 anchored a couple of miles away. I didn't understand why they were so offish. I didn't understand Dyer. For two vessels that had been advised to run in consort, Dyer had made no effort to discuss the advantages of the plan. After the cold shoulder he gave me in response to the favor I had done getting him out of custody in Panama, I had no inclination to talk with him. We were two ships in the night.

When the anchor was on board, we took off across the Yucatan Channel with no more than a couple of peeps of air horn to announce our departure.

The current flowing north came at us like a jet as we approached the channel. It was a day's run to Mujeres Island. We headed southeast to compensate for the current. We had every expectation of raising Mujeres Island before darkness.

107

The wind was dead astern, and the tug behaved herself despite the heavy flow of water that would change its name to Gulf Stream as soon as it passed the Cape.

I got to thinking about the fishing vessel that had passed us going east and my own little vessel languishing in a boat yard in Fort Lauderdale. I began to develop a measure of anxiety about the chances we had of making a safe passage in the lifeboat, which lay in chocks on the boat deck, if we were forced to abandon the tug.

To begin with, the thing had no keel. The rudder was miniscule. The boat was supplied with a sail, which was fine if the wind was in the proper quarter and a likely landfall was straight down wind. But what of coral reefs lying offshore? What of the currents and the winds that were determined to drag you seaward? Kidd was on my watch in the morning. I shared my misgivings with him.

"Kidd," I said, "Do you remember those three pieces of dunnage that I asked you to pick up on the dock in Havana?"

"Yes sir."

"Get some of the boys who are off watch to come up here. I want to lift that lifeboat up on its davits about a foot high."

Kidd left the pilothouse and I took the wheel. Part of the crew came up on the boat deck, and they tried to lift that impossible tub. It was no use. It took the whole crew, including Namb and W. D. hauling on the falls, to get it up in the air.

"Now," I said to Kidd, "I want you to take those three boards, use two of them as a clamp and build a keel for that lifeboat."

Kidd was a carpenter. He went to work and built a keel that one could fasten to the one-inch strip that served as a keel. A single ten-penny nail was all that was needed to hold that keel in place. Kidd found a piece of plywood in the forward locker and doubled the size of the rudder.

We removed the keel, lowered the lifeboat back on its chocks, and kept the keel in readiness for the hour of disaster.

15

The wind came around astern of us by mid-morning, and the tug battled a confused sea until noon, by which time we had passed the most vehement section of the current. I rigged a lure with a piece of white toweling, a hook with a leader, and a couple hundred feet of quarter-inch manila. We caught bonitas. I had heard of natives down this way who ate them. They were too bloody for our taste. They impaled themselves on the hook with a tiresome regularity when suddenly the dolphin struck. Buster was out on the after-end of the boat deck barking his fool head off.

I had the line rigged the way Captain Erbe did, with a snatch block lashed halfway between the boat deck railing and the transom. When the dolphin hit, the hook and the snatch block jumped like a thing alive. We ran aft and hauled in the fish. It was a beauty, and we watched as I had done on another occasion as the brilliant colors like a flamboyant symbol left the fish and it lay inert and colorless on the steel deck.

W. D. was not the cook that Napoleon was, but he did a fair job of baking our prize, and we ate it with none of the misery and the tension that Napoleon invariably supplied.

It was afternoon when the low outline of Mujeres Island came into view. At first, there were faint dots along the horizon, and slowly they grew downward into trees, and finally the heartening evidence of surf and shoreline became apparent through the glass.

We found a kind of sea buoy, and we could see the houses on the island. We had no chart of the harbor, and we had no idea about whether the channel—if there was such a thing—was navigable for our nine feet of draft. The water was of a remarkable clarity, and I thought that it was worth the gamble to get as close to the town as possible.

Eddie got out on the bow with a sounding line and we headed in.

Eddie shouted the depths. "Twenty feet, fifteen feet, twelve feet, eighteen feet, eighteen feet, twenty feet"; and then, as we came to within half a mile of the stone pier that jutted out from the settlement, it was, "Twelve feet, fourteen feet, eleven feet."

That was my number, and I rang the telegraph, "half astern."

I rang to stop the engine, and Eddie lowered away the hook that was hanging ready on the davit at the bow. We were going to have to launch the lifeboat. The crew was spoiling to get ashore. They gathered on the boat deck and hauled on one fall, made it fast, and then hauled on the other. When the lifeboat was in the air, I said, "Kidd, will you please fasten the keel?"

Kidd dragged out the makeshift boards he had fastened together and lifted it up to the bottom of the boat. I held it up while he slipped that nail into the drilled hole.

"Now, my friends," I said, "we have a sailing vessel."

The crew swung the davits out over the side and lowered the boat away. Then they all scrambled down the ladder and jumped aboard the boat. Eddie was standing in the bow of the tug with the painter in his hand, waiting for me to go aboard the boat. I lowered Buster down from the boat deck, and he took his place in the stern as befits the master's dog. I went aboard and shipped the tiller. Then I asked the crew to break out the sail. It was dragged out from under their feet and stepped in the forward thwart. I directed Eddie, who had taken his place in the bow, to lash the boathook to the thwart, extending it forward to serve as a bowsprit.

Eddie didn't know quite what I meant. I wove through the nine men who were crowded into the boat, with Buster hard on my heels battling to stay with me. Up forward, I lashed down the boathook as a bowsprit and fastened the luff of the jib to the bitter end of it.

Then I struggled back through the crowd to my place at the tiller with Buster right behind me. "Now you may raise the mainsail and the jib."

Kidd pulled it up on its tiny sheave, and I held the sheet as she gathered way. The town was to the windward. We headed out on a starboard tack, and after about a half an

hour we were scarcely forty feet closer to the town dock than we were when we left the tug.

"Eddie," I said, "Perhaps that jib is too far out over the bow. Would you mind making that boathook loose and lashing it down so it does not protrude so far out?"

Eddie tore the lashing off and brought the boathook further inboard, which meant that Peacock had to move aside so that it could be made fast to the thwart that he was sitting on.

While this was taking place I said, "What we are trying to find out is whether this boat can be sailed to windward in case we have to abandon the tug on a lee coast."

To the nine men who were spoiling to get ashore for a bottle of beer or to find a woman, my preoccupation with sailing to windward didn't make a damn bit of sense. The boathook was lashed down in a more conventional position and off we went again.

The result was no more dramatic than the initial attempt. I decided to have one more try at getting that ornery tub to tack and to explain the necessity of such an advantage. When I brought the boat up into the wind to readjust the jib, Virgilio Varga, who had a low threshold for delay, spoke up.

"Captain," he said, "the trouble with you is that you fawk around too much."

There was a silence. No one said a word. The moment passed like an eternity. I thought of all the friends I had alienated over the years, the women who had abandoned the idea of sharing any kind of rational life with me. I thought of all opportunities for social intercourse that I had abnegated in my single-minded obsession with sailing boats.

I thought of my all-consuming passion for *Princess*, which had turned me into a kind of sea-going recluse. It hit me like an avalanche.

There was no recourse, no explanation was possible about the wonder of my way of life, about the grandeur of the sea, the evanescent sky. I looked around at nine pairs of eyes that were like the eyes of a ten-man jury waiting for the last holdout to speak his piece.

There was no way to turn. The whole manner of my life was on the line. I had to admit it. I did "fawk around" too much.

The verdict was in. Like a judge facing a habitual and unrepentant offender, I pronounced sentence on myself.

"Lower the sail and row her in," I said.

16

We landed on Mujeres Island four hundred years after the Conquistadors. No one met us at the dock.

When the Conquistadors landed, the entire male population fled in panic, fearing for their lives. *Mujeres* is the Spanish word for women.

When we came ashore, the population of Mujeres Island was predominantly male. There were no bars and no brothels. Ricky spoke to one of the natives and found out that a vessel that came to Mujeres Island every Saturday morning brought a number of public women. It was Monday, and the men on the island were content to wait.

There was some warm Mexican beer in a kind of general store and a matinee movie, with the sound blaring in Spanish, in an old stone building that doubled for the town hall. Ricky and I walked around the island. There were some banana trees, and on the north side of the island a coconut plantation. The owner of the plantation came running out to us. Ricky spoke with him in his native tongue. He was quite agitated.

Some of the boys off our vessel had been there. They climbed the trees and made off with some of the coconuts, which were green. The planter did not understand how a thing like that could have happened. I handed Ricky some money to give to the plantation owner. The man refused the money. The Mayans are a proud and gentle people.

It was the old story of the arrogant American. History had repeated itself. The Conquistadors were arrogant. They were not content with coconuts, they were after gold.

There was gold on that island, developers' gold. I could see it in the golden beach that ringed it. I could sense it in the luxuriant movement of the palm fronds in the east wind. The island was on the northernmost tip of Yucatan that reached up toward the tourist trade and the American dollar. Maybe the planter knew that there was gold on that island.

The crew wandered around. There was no action and so they gathered at the dock ready to go back aboard the tug.

We sailed back. With the wind abaft the beam we made good time. After the men had boarded the tug, Eddie, Kidd, and I stayed aboard the lifeboat with Buster. After a few more adjustments, such as stepping the mast further aft, we managed to get the boat to run a point or so into the wind. It proved that we could make it against an onshore wind.

In the morning the ST250 stood out to sea. We sounded our way gingerly across the lacework of shoals and intervening sandbars and headed out for open water.

It was a short run to the island of Cozumel. We sighted the lighthouse before noon and took the inside passage on the western side of the island, which was protected from the weather. We dropped our kedge anchor alongside a little town in the clearest water in the world.

The anchor went down sixty feet before it hit bottom. We paid out a lot of cable to make sure that she wouldn't drag in the current that swept up along the island. You could see the bottom as clearly as you could see the palm of your hand.

After we had lunch and Namb had finished washing the dishes, he asked me if he could borrow the little grappling

116

hook that was in the forward lazarette. He had a ball of fishing line to fasten it to. I said, "Sure, go get it." I had no idea what he wanted it for. I went up in my cabin and took a nap.

I woke up when Buster started barking. Namb was up in the bow flinging that grappling over the side. Every time he flung the grappling, Buster would bark. There must have been some retriever in him. I came down from the pilothouse to watch.

Time after time Namb would swing that grappling out and then he would haul it in.

"What are you doing, Namb?"

"There is an old anchor down there. I am trying to pick it up."

I looked over the side. I could see all kinds of fish swimming by, hundreds of them. There were barracuda, shark, parrot fish, yellow tails, and below them was the anchor that Namb was trying to salvage as a souvenir.

"Namb," I said as gently as possible, "that anchor you are trying to pick up is not an old anchor. It is our anchor. It is down sixty feet and it weighs five hundred pounds. I doubt whether you will be able to raise it with that little hook and that shoestring. The water is very clear and that anchor appears to be within arm's reach. See those fish down there?"

Namb stared over the side through his thick glasses.

"Some of them are swimming more than forty feet below us. They are much bigger than they look and so is the anchor. Don't fall over the side or the fish will have you for dinner."

A native skiff came by and some of us went ashore, which saved us from the Herculean task of launching the lifeboat.

There was a dilapidated little bar in town and some tired-looking natives with bare feet shuffling around the earthern floor. Dogs were scratching fleas and contending with the flies along the wall of the building. They looked diseased. I was glad that I had left Buster on the tug. I had given him a bath, and I didn't want him associating with the raunchy dogs in Cozumel.

Buster had become a kind of one-man dog. He tolerated being petted by the crew, but he showed a special kind of affection for me, despite the fact that it was W. D. who fed him. But Buster was not the possessive type of one-man dog. He did not hanker to go ashore when I did.

The fat bartender with a cigar in his face opened a bottle of warm beer for me and continued to stare into space. They were building an airfield on the northern end of the island, and the workmen came into town at the end of the day and hung around the bar. Eddie did a land-office business, selling cigarettes to them at the equivalent of a dollar a pack.

When I got back to the vessel, Namb had substituted a fish hook for the grapnel, and after experimenting with several kinds of bait from the galley, he had managed to catch several red snappers and some yellowtails. He said, "I caught more fish for the other fish than I caught for myself."

Anyway, we had fish for dinner and so, evidently, did the big fish down below. In the morning we raised the hook, and after Peacock got enough compressed air in the tank to start the diesel, we turned and headed down along the treacherous coast toward Honduras.

By noon we were abeam of the reef at Turneffe where a T49 had run aground and broken up. It would have happened to Captain Larry as well if I hadn't cautioned him about skirting that miserable menace to shipping.

The reef at Turneffe stretches for miles along that coast. Its outlying coral pinnacles are loosely charted on the map, which is based on British Admiralty surveys done a hundred years ago. We ran the inside channel, giving it a wide berth. The captain of the T49 was lucky enough to be rescued by a shoal draft fishing vessel; I saw him in Lew Higgins's office after he had returned to New Orleans. He was sitting there with his head in his hands. I never found out whether the rest of his crew were lucky enough to make it. Higgins just stared at me when I asked.

As we passed down in that tranquil sea between Turneffe and the mainland we made no effort to spot the wreck of Captain Larry's sister ship. We were happy enough to get out of sight of that maritime graveyard in one piece.

As the afternoon wore on, Eddie and I were in the pilothouse when we raised a tiny spot on the horizon. We had the chart spread out on the table behind the wheel, and while Eddie held the tug on course, I identified the spot, which slowly bled down into a palm tree and then a tiny grove of palm trees. It was Southwest Key, which lies off the coast of British Honduras.

I took the wheel as Eddie studied the chart. He was all excited. "Do you suppose we could stop there, Captain?"

I looked at Eddie. "I didn't figure you for a romantic, Eddie, I thought that you were a hard-boiled seaman."

"There ain't no such animal," said Eddie.

"You know damn well that we are going to stop at Southwest Key." I said.

Eddie took the helm again as I studied the chart. There were two crosses indicating coral heads that were disposed in a northwesterly direction from the key. Gradually, we ran south and east till the point of the island was due north of us. Then we ran northwest in a line parallel to the coral heads.

When I was sure that we had passed the vicinity of the obstruction, we turned and ran northeast for a half a mile.

Eddie was now out on the bow with a sounding line. There was plenty of water below us. I said to Eddie from the pilothouse window, "Keep your eyes open, Eddie, and sing out if you begin to see a shoal area. If we are going to tear the bottom out of her, to hell with the island."

Eddie smiled up at me. We understood each other. We were a couple of crazy romantics, but not crazy enough to wind up in fiddler's green.

At the end of the half-mile run to the northeast, I made a

right-angle turn and came slowly in out of the northwest, heading southeast true.

Eddie kept sounding away. There was a clear passage right up to within a hundred feet of the loveliest cove you have ever imagined. We dropped the hook.

A black man came out in a punt. There were two men on the island and an old lady staring at us from the knoll beyond the silver beach.

The black man sculling with one hand said to me when I came down from the pilothouse, "You must have come in here before."

I shook my head. "I don't believe it," he continued, "You must have been here before. You came in as if you knew."

"I have a chart," I said. "I believe the chart."

"You came in perfect."

"Thank you."

"You might have come in this way," he said pointing to the open water between the south point of the island and the direction of the closest coral pinnacle to the southwest.

"Next time I will know."

There was a next time. Years later I came down by plane and was ferried out to this magical place by a Frenchman who had been variously a lawyer in Paris, a taxidermist in Denver, and who was presently the operator of a scuba-diving resort on an island adjacent to Southwest Key.

It wasn't the same. There is a personal intimacy about an island. It is the same thing that is offered by a beautiful woman. Love can't be warmed over. I had been in love with that island.

We launched the lifeboat and we all went ashore, landing on the white beach in the cove. During high water the island was two islands, which became one as the tide receded. There was a high knoll on its southern end and a stand of coconut palms. There were some scattered palms on the northern part.

We met the sweet old lady, who spoke with a Scottish

accent, and her two sons. The old man was her paramour. There was a little pet pig named Willie who followed her around, trying his damnedest to make like a dog. Thank God Buster didn't come ashore. Buster was partial to pork chops.

The crew took a quick look around and went back aboard the tug. I stayed on the island.

I sat on the curved trunk of a coconut palm before a blazing fire as the night followed an appropriately dramatic sunset. The old lady spoke of their life together on the island, and her sons husked coconuts by slamming them down on a pointed stake driven into the ground near the fire. The husks were fed to the fire, and the little pig snorted and frolicked in the warmth of it.

"It is forty miles," she said, "to Belize. We make the trip once a month with a thousand coconuts, and we take Willie along.

"What do you get for the coconuts?"

"We get a penny a piece. With the ten dollars I can buy enough flour and oil to last us for a month. Our needs are simple."

There was a tiny shack on the knoll where they kept their possessions. They slept under the stars. They drank rain water and coconut milk and they were all lean and fit. When I compared it to the way the average American lives, it boggled the mind. Here was a tiny segment of peace in a world lacerated by conflict.

I spoke of the war, which they had heard about in Belize. It seemed incomprehensible to them. Watching the stabbing light of stars a million light-years away through the slowly moving fronds, war seemed just as incomprehensible to me. The old lady went on about her life on the mainland.

"You evidently don't care for it in Belize."

"It is dirty in Belize."

I found out years later how right the old lady was. The sewers are open ditches in Belize, and typhoid is as prevalent as the common cold. They had found their nirvana, and I was fiercely envious. I could see *Princess*, my sloop, in dreamy reflection in the still water of the cove.

I tasted broiled lobster that the old lady prepared and heart of palm that was a triumphant salad. I broke bread that had the fragrance of coconut with these quiet, happy people.

"I ferment the coconut for yeast," she said, "and I bake the bread before the fire with that piece of tin."

The bread was light and tasty. I was told about the thousands of lobsters in the cove and the endless variety of seafood. They had turtle eggs and turtle meat. They wanted for nothing. The old lady spoke laughingly about her errands to the north part of the island, with the little pig swimming after her as she waded across the shallows. In my mind's eye I could see the sunlit days, the soft windswept nights, the ultimate contentment of their life on that precious isolated acre. I thought about it when in 1955 I heard of the hurricane and the monstrous tidal wave that for hours buried that island under the sea.

I never was able to find out whether they survived. In the time that I was with them, their lives seemed removed from this world, and eternal.

I whistled for Eddie, and he came and got me in the lifeboat.

It might have been a disservice to the family who lived on Southwest Key, but later that night I gathered up all the woman's service magazines, the *Ladies' Home Journal,* the *Woman's Home Companion, Family Circle,* piled them into the lifeboat with a hefty load of tinned hams and canned whatnots, and rowed out to the island with a cargo from the so-called civilized world.

I wanted the old lady to know how much garbage she had skipped by choosing to live on Southwest Key.

The magazines had been brought lovingly aboard before we sailed by some misguided members of the New Orleans chapter of the American Red Cross. I was glad to get rid of them.

They were evidently not too disturbed by that reminder of our way of life. The old man had an enormous brace of lobsters and two loaves of that superb coconut-flavored bread for us as we were about to haul the anchor and shove off.

I thanked the old man and said goodbye. Before we left, I offered him several cartons of cigarettes as a final parting gift.

He smiled and thanked me kindly, but he turned them down. He said that he had no use for them. Eddie stared at him. Eddie was a chain-smoker.

With the anchor aweigh, we chugged out through the passage the old man had pointed out, and we followed a course toward Puerto Barrios, which lies in the western right-angle corner of the Houduranian countries.

I stood on the after boat deck with Buster as four tiny figures waved to us from the knoll on Southwest Key, and soon sank behind the great round hill of water that lies at the top of the world and is known as the horizon.

17

We had an early start. We had left Southwest Key just after dawn. The sea was smooth and we had a gentle breeze that favored us. As we headed down into the Gulf of Honduras, I decided to skip Puerto Barrios and try to make Porto Béllo by dusk.

There was no reason to stop at Puerto Barrios. I had been there on the little T-boat with Captain Larry. I remembered the place. There was an endless line of flatcars loaded with bananas that were being stowed aboard a ship. There was a line of shanty houses along the tracks, and as the train came through, some of the natives jumped aboard and tossed a couple of huge bunches on the ground; the bananas were whisked away by their confederates. For a country that has the richest productivity per square mile in the world, the Honduranian Republic has a disgraceful degree of poverty. There was lumber, Honduras mahogany grew there like weeds. There was gold in the rivers, and silver. Bananas were coming out of their ears. Everything was controlled by a few fat cats among the natives and the foreign corporations. The average Honduranian was muttering about revolution. He was broke and he was hungry. I decided to give the place a wide berth.

We sighted the imposing tops of the blue mountains long before we sighted land. We made the turn between the islands of Utila and Roatán and ran along the lee of Roatán as the northwest wind began to pipe up.

It was a peaceful passage until Namb started hollering down on the main deck.

I rang the telegraph to stop the engine. When I looked over the side, Namb was running around the deck with blood coming out of his pants leg. I saw Eddie down there. He was doubled up laughing

"What the hell is going on down there?"

"It's nothing, Captain, Numb has got the monthlies," and then he started laughing again.

"You guys are a pain in the ass," I said. Virgilio came up to the pilothouse.

"It is nothing," he said. "Somebody poured a bottle of ketchup in his pants."

I rang the telegraph, "full ahead." It grew late in the afternoon. I did not relish coming into Porto Béllo in the hours of darkness. We had run out of the protection of the island of Roatán, and the tug was wallowing in the trough of the sea.

I called Eddie up to the pilothouse. When he came up the ladder there was a silly grin on his face. "Now look Eddie, you are the executive officer of this vessel. I am depending on you to maintain discipline."

"Yes sir," said Eddie.

I had to smile. "You know this goddamn trap could turn over and drown every bastard on board while you guys are farting around pouring ketchup in people's pants."

"Yes sir," said Eddie.

I turned away from Eddie and looked at the chart.

"Do you know what it says here?" I said to Eddie.

"What's that Captain?"

"It says that the island of Roatán has been reported to lie five miles to the east of its position on the chart."

"Isn't that a hell of a note," said Eddie. "If they moved it over to where it is supposed to be we would have five more miles of protection from the weather."

"We will leave the island where it is, wherever it is, and you go on down and tell that crazy gang to leave Namb alone."

"Yes sir," said Eddie.

I could hear them laughing down below.

We came into the ancient port of Porto Béllo, now called Trujillo, at that fortuitous time of day when it is just dark enough to identify the aids to navigation and still light enough to judge the distance and to sense the mystery of a strange port. Coming in at night is like bumping around blind. If you follow the lights, you know that you are going to make it, and yet it takes all the nerve you have to believe.

There is a great arm of land that shields the entrance of the harbor from the prevalent northerly. We tied up alongside right next to the ST249, which had arrived that afternoon.

I had read about this port. I had heard about the great slide that had dumped half the town into the sea during an earthquake. I had known about the pirates who frequented this secure harbor, about Morgan and Blackbeard and all the rest of the cutthroats.

W. D., who had been hanging on by his teeth during the last hours of that passage, managed to assemble some sort of a supper. Sitting there in silence at the head of the galley table and looking down along the line of faces, I wondered whether I had the same kind of men on the ST250 as Morgan had, or Blackbeard. Raiding innocent merchantmen and cutting throats was a far cry from pouring ketchup down a man's pants, but suddenly I realized that this gang would have no difficulty making the transition.

There was a United States Navy office in town. I went over to get my clearance to sail the following day. I was instructed to leave at eight o'clock the next morning in company with the ST249. They had been given the same instructions.

I went ashore with the crew and we had a beer or two in the local pub. There wasn't much to do and I hit the sack early. It had been a long day at sea.

I got up at half-past seven the next morning, stretched, yawned, and looked out of the port. The ST249 was gone. I went down on the dock and spoke to the harbor master.

"Where the hell is the ST249? You know, the other Army tugboat."

"Ah," said the dockmaster, "She left at four o'clock this morning."

"She was supposed to leave when we did."

"Oh, no," said the dockmaster. "She sailed out of here at four o'clock this morning."

I went back aboard my vessel. Eddie was in the pilothouse. "Eddie," I said, "That crazy bastard Dyer on the ST249 has decided to make a race of it. He left this morning at four o'clock."

"You've got to be kidding."

"Take a look."

Eddie looked out of the pilothouse window to where the ST249 had been. "She's gone all right."

"He wants to beat our time to Panama."

"Let's go," said Eddie.

18

We left in such a hurry that we forgot the dog. We made a fast turn in the harbor and went back alongside to pick up Buster, who had gone for a constitutional down along the dock. We saw him playing with some kids.

Buster was all smiles when we picked him up. He smiled with his tail and kept a straight face as much as to say, "You know there is a law about abandoning seamen in a foreign port."

We shoved off again and the race was on. The wind was still strong out of the northeast, but with Peacock down below and that Enterprise diesel, we felt that we had an even chance of overtaking the ST249 before we got to Panama.

In good conscience I could understand Dyer taking off at dawn. It was a long run to Bragman's Bluff or Puerto Cabezas, as it is now called, and an even longer run to Limón. Dyer had no intention of getting trapped by nightfall and the blind lighthouse on Cape Gracias à Dios, to say nothing of Miskito Channel. What bugged me is why he shoved off like a thief in the night.

The question of whether Dyer was determined to make a score by beating us to Panama or by the less admirable expedient of hoping for a disastrous capsize or grounding of the ST250, was beside the point. We were out to win the race and teach him a lesson. Peacock revved her up and we were clicking off the miles despite the growing intensity of the northeaster which had sown the sea with whitecaps all down along the coast.

By midday the wind had shifted somewhat to the east and increased in intensity. The vessel was diving so badly that I had to slow her down. She would lift and plow under, taking more green water on the lower deck than the scuppers were able to handle. With the extra weight of water swarming around the deck, there was the ever-present danger of a sudden broadside wave that would turn us over.

It was imperative to cut her speed. The notion of overtaking our companion tug was abandoned. We crawled along that inhospitable coast until darkness began to set in.

I had been poring over the chart, trying to find a place to run in out of the ferocity of the weather. The coastline presented no harbor of refuge. There were inlets and bays that were a boon to shoal draft boats, but the reefs and the shoals allowed no possibility of accomodation for a vessel that drew nine feet.

We came to a place right outside of one of the shoal inlets that showed twenty feet of water.

"Eddie," I said, "you better get that davit ready and take the lashings off the anchor. We are going to have to sweat it out right here all night."

Kidd said, "I'll go down and help you, Eddie."

I backed the engine and put her stern to the sea so that the men could work on the bow without being swamped. When they were ready to let the anchor go I rang the telegraph "slow ahead" and turned into the wind. When we faced the wind Eddie let her go. He paid out fifty fathoms of cable and Kidd bound up the line with chaffing gear where it passed through the hawsepipe of the vessel.

It was a long night. There had to be a man on watch at all

times. The tug would lift with the sea and plunge and roll. Water seeped into the cabins below, and the men climbed up into the pilothouse and dozed on the deck. The extra weight of the crew in the pilothouse did nothing to help the center of gravity of the tug, and she wallowed precariously in the darkness.

At one point, a vicious wave rolled her so badly that it seemed certain that she would founder right at anchor. At that moment I thought about Dyer and wondered whether he really wanted to see us go down. I tried to dismiss the idea as generated by frustration and fear, but the more I thought about it the more convinced I became that there was something devilish about him.

Dawn came up like some kind of last-minute reprieve, and the wind moderated, as it often does at sunrise or sunset. This gave us the opportunity to take in the slack of the cable and weigh anchor without more than a spray of brine on our backs.

We were underway early, with a good chance of making Puerto Cabezas, which lay around the Cape Gracias á Dios, by dusk.

When the men had the anchor aboard and the cable faked down, Eddie came up into the pilothouse.

"Eddie," I said, "I don't know a hell-of-a-lot about sin and retribution, but there is one crime that you committed that the heavenly father has got to overlook. As the instigator of that crime I know he has forgiven me."

"You mean the time I swapped that Navy anchor for a kedge?" asked Eddie.

"That's the one, Eddie." I said. "That was a beautiful crime. Go, and sin no more."

"I'd do it again," said Eddie.

19

It was Buster who noticed it first. He had been trying to tell me about it. I didn't hear him. Sometimes you don't listen to a dog.

Buster was not the complaining type. Maybe he thought that it was one of those things that happen on a tugboat and that maybe it would go away by itself. It shook the hell out of him.

It didn't go away. It got worse. It started as a faint vibration. He must have been the only one who felt it. He lost a few days sleep over it, but he made it up at night, when the engine down below stopped running.

Now that the engine was running all the time as we rounded Cape Gracias à Dios, it began to get to him. He would get up off the deck, put his muzzle in my hand, and whine gently. As we passed through Miskito Channel, I began to sense the vibration myself. I asked the chief engineer about it.

"I have been trying to track it down," said Peacock. "Either the engine has shifted on its bed, which would create a misalignment with the drive shaft, or else the propeller is bent. You don't remember hitting anything, do you?"

"No," I said.

"A derelict or a piece of wreckage?"

"No."

"Then it has to be the engine."

I tried to explain that to Buster. It was beyond his ken. He didn't know what I was talking about. All he knew was that the deck was shaking worse all the time and that it was useless to try to get some shut-eye with that vibration going on.

Despite the shakes, the engine kept right on spinning out its revolutions and by nightfall we drew into Puerto Cabezas. There is a long pier at Puerto Cabezas that extends almost a quarter of a mile out into deep water from a completely unprotected shoreline. There are some reefs and coral shoals that are part of the jeopardy of Miskito Channel, which does offer some insulation against a northeaster. When the wind howls up out of the south and opposes the current, all hell breaks loose.

The current runs so fast in a southerly direction along that coast that it is wise to simply put a bite of the anchor cable on a piling on the dock and let the vessel float free as if at a mooring. The current runs continually night and day and is unaffected by the tide. It is a tightrope act to get ashore, but that was no problem. We had a full crew of acrobats. Buster stayed on board.

I left the deckhand on watch with Buster for company, and most of us went ashore after supper. We climbed the hill to the shanty barroom, and the proprietor greeted us with the same crooked smile that I remembered when I came there as mate on the tug commanded by Lawson. There was something different now about his smile. The tooth with the gold cap was missing.

And so was the little brown public woman with the ponytail. I learned that she had taken up with a planter back in the hills; she had achieved the distinction of becoming a private woman. It was a sad thing for me and for the public at large. I lifted a warm bottle of beer in a private and silent toast to her memory.

20

After we passed Cape Gracias à Dios, the wind moderated and the sky was clear. It looked like we were in for a spell of fair weather. The vibration in the engine started in the morning. With the promise of a calm sea all we had to worry about now was the possibility of a mechanical breakdown or submarine action.

We had been lucky so far. We had not heard a single roar of a gun blast or the staccato of machine-gun fire. No torpedoes had been directed at us, and our enemy so far had been the mercurial sea. Now, it was also the withering, blurring illness of the engine that bugged us. We kept going.

With the engine running and the bite of the cable that held us to the dock made loose, we turned and headed down toward Limón.

Except for the irritation of the engine, it was a pleasant run. There were scattered clouds, and for early February it was as warm as summertime in New Orleans.

Kidd was at the wheel with a watchful eye on the binnacle when he called me into the pilothouse. "Captain," he said, "take a look at the compass."

I walked over to the binnacle and stared. The compass card was spinning as if it was hooked up to an electric motor.

"Now what the hell is going on?"

"I'll be damned if I know," said Kidd.

There was a powerful smell of alcohol in the pilothouse.

"See that cloud right over the bow," I said to Kidd. "Steer for that cloud."

I whistled for Peacock in the speaking tube. "What do you want?" he answered.

"I want you to come up to the pilothouse."

Peacock swung up the side ladder and came into the pilothouse. "Take a peek into that binnacle," I said.

Peacock stared at the compass spinning like an electric fan. His jaw hung down and he rubbed his eyes. "I'll be a son of a bitch," he said.

Eddie came up out of the galley where he was having coffee and stared at the compass. "Eddie," I said, "you better get the box compass out of the lifeboat."

Eddie came back with it as soon as he could unfasten the lashings that held the tarpaulin cover on the boat. I knew from the cloud that Kidd was holding the vessel heads-on and that the box compass was so deviated as to make it useless. All that magnetic material of which the pilothouse was constructed made the lifeboat compass a cockeyed liar. The men glanced around with a feeling of helplessness.

"Don't worry about it," I assured them. "We'll get to Limón."

I had a copy of the Hydrographic Office publication called *Azimuths of the Sun.* Our hack watch was set to Greenwich time. The watch was not accurate enough to ascertain a decent longitude, but it was close enough to give us some idea of the direction we had to go.

Thank God the sun was shining. If it had been overcast we would still be out there trying to figure where to steer if we wanted to go south.

With the engine shaking the bejesus out of the little ship, we were certainly interested in sailing south. I worked out an azimuth of the sun and found that she bore some ten degrees west of south. By subtracting that ten degrees from the bearing of the sun, I got a pretty close approximation of where south was hiding. I picked out a cloud on the horizon that was ten degrees east of the bearing of the sun, and I had Kidd steer for that cloud.

Clouds move. So does the sun. There was a gentle breeze from the east, and I kept having to work out new azimuths every ten minutes all afternoon.

After the sun went down, I went around to the stern of the vessel. Standing on the boat deck, I tried to find the north star. Now we were sailing blind.

We had traveled far south. The north star was so close to the horizon as to be barely visible. Fortunately, the Dipper was high in the sky and the pointers, which define the drinking edge of the dipper, put the finger on the approximate position of Polaris.

Eddie was on the wheel now, and I told him to turn around and steer with his eye on the dipper. We zigzagged all over the sea. Generally, we headed south.

We worked our way down to the vicinity of Limón the way Buster might find his way back home or the way the Canadian geese, with their mysterious equipment, can instinctively find their way to a familiar breeding ground.

The loom of the lights indicating the direction of a city is a faint glow on the horizon that gladdens the heart. We directed our course toward that glow, and the shiver of the ship as the engine strained against the misalignment of her bearings was like the shiver of excitement at the moment that danger has passed.

The lights of the city, like a row of jewels, popped into view. The entrance into the harbor is tricky, especially without a compass. We cut the engine and signalled for a pilot.

The signal light was on top of the pilothouse. There was a

136

handle that directed the powerful beam, which extended down through the overhead. I directed the beam at the center of the town and signalled the international code letter for a pilot. It was the letter *P*, a short flash, a long flash, and two short flashes. I repeated the signal for several minutes. There was no answering signal from the town.

Then I spelled out *pilot* in code. Still no answer. I kept this up for close to a quarter of an hour and there was no response whatsoever.

I said to Eddie, "What in hell do you suppose is going on in that town?"

Eddie shook his head and puffed on a cigarette.

"There has got to be a pilot in that place."

"Maybe he is out on a date with some chick."

"There has got to be more than one pilot in that town. Limón is a major port. Where in hell are they?"

Peacock came up into the pilothouse and stared at the town. "Why can't we run in?" he said.

I showed him the entrance to Limón on the chart. The channel runs right alongside an ugly reef for a long distance. "I would have to have the nerve of a brass monkey to attempt to run that channel with a compass in the dark. Without a compass I throw in the sponge."

"What are we going to do, hang around here all night?"

"I could bring her in closer. We will have to drop the hook."

I began to signal again. Finally, after another half hour of calling for a pilot with the signal, we unlimbered the massive searchlight and threw a blinding light on the town. Then in exasperation we turned on every light on the vessel till she must have appeared like a birthday cake.

"That ought to bring them out," said Eddie.

It didn't bring them out. It turned the town into a seething panic. Not less than a month before, an enemy submarine had directed a torpedo down along that entrance channel and had blown a five-thousand-ton ship to hell and gone right at the dock. To the people in the town, the frightening lights of the ST250 were a sure indication that an invasion of the town was underway.

The local police were directing measures to repel the invasion. The ancient French 75-millimeter cannon that had been a decoration in the town square for a hundred years was wheeled out on the parapet, and men were scurrying around looking for powder and cannon balls.

The citizenry of Limón were rounding up every rifle, every fowling piece, every pistol they could lay their hands on, and were passing them out to every able-bodied man in a valiant effort to defend the town at any cost. The women and the children were being shepherded to a comparatively safe place deep in the town. Some of the more affluent families had already taken off into the hills.

When Captain Dyer staggered out of a bar and looked around, he couldn't believe what was going on. He looked out over the parapet to a cluster of lights that resembled the configuration of lights on the ST249. Suddenly it hit him. The lights out there beyond the reef were the lights of the ST250.

Dyer staggered over to the chief of police waving his arm. "No invasion," he said. "No invasion."

The chief of police looked at him. "No invasion?"

"Si," said Dyer. "No invasion. American tugboat."

Panic vanished as suddenly as it appeared. A pilot was dispatched, and the pilot boat arrived at the ST250 at two o'clock in the morning.

For the invader and the invaded it had been a long night.

It looked like we were in for a prolonged visit. There were no facilities to repair a compass in Limón. A captain had to be crazy to go to sea without one.

A message had been sent by the local consul to Panama apprising the Army authorities of our predicament. Peacock was ready to chance it with the engine, which was acting like it had St. Vitus dance. Without a compass we were really hog-tied.

Limón was not much of a town for a sailor. There were a couple of bars, but not much action. I walked off the tug and passed by a huge estate, which was fenced with fancy iron-work. There was a bench outside the gate and a chic-looking babe having her shoes shined by a little black boy.

I sat next to her and watched the operation. He could sure snap that shoeshine rag.

The girl, her shoes shining like her eyes, got up and went into the compound.

"Nice girl," I said to the boy. "Bonita."

"Si", he answered. "It is the governor's daughter. I shine her shoes every day. I like that. She has no pants on. Very nice."

I smiled and went on into town.

I walked into the stores, and I walked around the town, and almost everywhere I went that smart little Spanish gal, who found it too hot to wear panties, would show up with her mama in tow.

I had to pay my respects to the American consul. He had recently been transferred from a similar post in Havana. We talked about the old city, and he asked me if we had heard some explosions in the vicinity of Puerto Cabezas and around the cape in Trujillo.

"We heard nothing."

"A destroyer and some planes were depth charging. Some enemy subs had been sighted. I guess you were lucky to get out of that area when you did."

"I was luckier than you know," I said, thinking about that wild night off the cape when we lay at anchor.

As I was about to leave the consulate, who shows up but the governor's daughter, sans panties and with her mama still in tow. We were formally introduced by the consul.

I would like to relate that a budding romance blossomed

139

in the sultry atmosphere of Limón, but that was hardly the case. She didn't speak enough English and I didn't speak enough Spanish to get past the formalities. She glanced at me enticingly and I stared at her. That was as far as it went. I began to regret having played hookey from Latin classes in high school. Social life was easier in the brothels. I bowed out.

I wound up in a bar down by the ships. I was having a beer alongside a huge black man with a beard whom the bartender addressed as "Captain."

"What kind of a ship are you the master of, Captain?"

"I have that little coastwise vessel at anchor off your tug."

"Where do you go from here?" I asked.

"Panama," he answered. I bought him a beer.

"When do you plan to leave?"

"Thursday morning. We shove off at four o'clock."

The wheels began to spin in my head. It was Tuesday. We were laid up waiting for a compass to be flown to Limón from Panama. It could be the duration before we got out of town.

From our point of view there was nothing wrong with taking a vacation in Limón. We were collecting double pay for lying in dangerous waters. As far as the war effort was concerned, it stank.

"How fast does your ship travel?" I asked the captain.

"Five knots is the best we can do."

Even with the engine on the ST250 shaking as if it had the ague we could keep up with that coaster. The ST249, knowing that we were disabled, showed every indication that she was anticipating a leisurely sojourn in Limón. Maybe I could still beat that bastard Dyer to Panama. I bought the captain another drink.

"Captain," I said, "do you know anything about Southwest Key?"

"Oh yes," he said, "It is a lovely island. It belongs to a man by the name of Hunter who lives in Belize."

"Do you suppose that he would sell it?"

"Yes, he will sell it. He wants seven hundred dollars for it," said the captain. "Would you like to buy it?"

"I was thinking about it," I said.

"It would be a nice place to live if you don't mind the rats."

"Are there rats on Southwest Key?"

"Didn't they tell you about them?"

"No."

"Some fisherman scuttled his vessel in the cove to get rid of them. They all swam ashore. They nest in the coconut palms. Someday there will come a hurricane and blow them all off the island."

"They didn't seem to bother the people who are living there now," I said.

"They are used to rats. They come from Belize. There are plenty of rats in Belize."

I bought another round of drinks, and I asked the captain of the coaster to keep my plan to follow him under his hat. He smiled and nodded, and I said good-night.

The next day was Wednesday. I saw Dyer strolling about the town as if he never heard of the war effort. That night I tipped the boys off about my plan to follow the coaster down to Panama, and I told Peacock to make sure he had enough compressed air in the tank to start the engine at dawn.

"And goddamn it, keep your mouths shut. I want everyone back on the tug by midnight."

They were all there at midnight including Buster, who had become acquainted with a shorthaired bitch with a body like a dachshund. He had made the supreme sacrifice, like Virgilio, who also found it difficult to get ahead of his heart. Silently, as the coaster coughed into life and made her way toward the channel, we slipped our lines and followed.

As we moved through the channel and followed the stern light of the coaster before the first light of day, it occurred to me that we were like the blind following the blind. I knew the kind of navigation practiced by the captain of the coaster. It was instinctive piloting practiced by many native captains along the coast. Their ignorance of celestial navigation was abysmal. With no compass aboard the ST250, we were obliged to follow.

Kidd was doing a good job keeping a respectful distance behind the vessel. It was a clear night, and I could tell from the position of the Big Dipper as I walked aft on the boat deck that we were headed generally in the direction of Panama. I began to think about the big jump across the Pacific which was becoming more imminent. What if I were lost over the side, or what if I was incapacitated? How would the crew ever find their way to a safe landfall?

There was a radio on board, but it had a limited range. Maybe fifty miles. Which direction would they travel? They could run out of fuel and water. The vessel carried a limited supply of food. I wondered whether they would turn cannibal and start eating each other. They would probably begin by having Namb for dinner. They had already prepared him with the ketchup. It was vital that I impart what knowledge I had of navigation to at least one member of the crew.

I had approached Eddie, the first officer, with the intention of teaching him to navigate. Eddie was a curious kind of student. He had little schooling. He was completely oblivious of the multiplication table, and his knowledge of simple addition consisted of counting on his fingers.

I tried starting at the beginning with Eddie. "How much is eight times eight?" I would say.

"Fifty-eight," Eddie would say, or "seventy-two," looking at me like a man with a rifle in a shooting gallery.

"You didn't hit it, Eddie," I would say. "This is not a guessing game. You have to know or figure it up."

I gave up on Eddie after a while. The curious thing about it was that when it came to playing casino Eddie was a whiz.

The second officer, Virgilio Varga, who was constantly pining for his lost love in New Orleans, was too preoccupied with himself to be interested in navigation. I didn't pursue the idea. The only member of the deck gang who had benefited from a rudimentary education was B. L. K. Kidd who was doing his trick at the wheel.

I started in on him. He ate it up. In five minutes in the dark while he was keeping the vessel on course, Kidd digested that part of the theory of navigation that relates to finding one's latitude by an observation of the sun at noon. When noon arrived the next day and we were slowly cutting down the mileage between ourselves and our objective, Kidd took the sextant, caught the sun on our meridian, and worked out a perfect latitude. I had a navigator on board!

By nightfall, we had followed the coaster down into the great dip in the isthmus known as the Gulf of the Mosquitoes. We ducked into the lee of a small island which is called Escudo de Veraguas right behind the coaster. The coaster's captain lowered a huge kedge anchor. When it came to ground tackle the native pilots didn't fool around with Navy anchors. We were invited to pass a mooring line to his stern.

Eddie was out on the bow with the heaving line. The monkey fist fell short into the water. Eddie wound up and tried again. After the fourth time I lost patience with Eddie, came down from the pilothouse, and threw the monkey fist myself. Then I was sorry about it. The tension was getting to me. Even Buster eyed me suspiciously when I came back into the pilothouse.

It had been a slow, tedious business tagging after the sluggish native vessel all day. The heat of the day had become oppressive. It would be a welcome relief to get through the canal and start heading north into a more moderate climate.

While we were moored to the coaster right after supper, a dugout skiff came alongside. The man in the boat, a native of Costa Rica who looked like an Indian, came aboard. There were great goings-on half the night, with Varga and some of

143

the crew going ashore in the dugout, back and forth till the small hours of the morning. I hit the sack and slept despite the ruckus down below.

I hopped out of the sack early the next morning to face the last segment of the long leg of our journey from New Orleans to Panama. The sun came up like a hot coal out of the caldron of the Caribbean. The captain of the coaster and his two-man crew were sweating at the anchor. They made loose our mooring line our engine took up where it left off in that dizzying cadence, and we followed in what seemed like an easterly direction.

It was a long day. The heat was oppressive and the vibration of the engine, which seemed to grow worse, had us all seeing double. Late in the afternoon, the faint haze of a coastline came into view, and at last, dead ahead of us, the sea buoy hove into sight.

The more exuberant members of the crew let out a whoop, I rang the telegraph "full ahead," and we proceeded into the harbor of Panama.

There was a long line of buoys approaching the harbor. A patrol vessel or pilot boat was standing in readiness before us. Just as we came up to take the pilot aboard, I looked astern. There was the ST249 coming in hell-for-leather behind us.

As we came close aboard the pilot vessel, a man with a megaphone shouted. "We will put a pilot aboard the vessel behind you. Follow him in."

I said to Eddie, "To hell with that noise."

They put a pilot on the ST249 and we stayed just ahead of our companion vessel all the way in.

We had beaten Dyer to Panama. As we rounded into the basin near the Gatun Lock, I still had the engine at half speed. I asked Eddie to get a heaving line ready as we came alongside.

Eddie went below for a moment and came swinging back

up the ladder to the wheelhouse. "Captain," he said, "we haven't got any heaving lines."

"Where in hell are they?"

"Virgilio swapped them for a bottle of booze last night on that island."

"I'll be damned." I jammed the wheel down hard left. I rang the telegraph "full astern."

Nothing happened. A whistle came back from the engine room on the speaking tube. It was Peacock. "We have no reverse," he shouted. "I can't get her to back up."

The vessel coming into the basin at nearly full bore headed for a resounding crash against the concrete wall dead ahead. We had enough way on her for steerage. She made a wide turn, barely scraping the three hard walls of the basin and came on out.

With the engine dead we came in gently on the second turn and made a sailboat landing. Kidd jumped ashore and hooked a bite of line around a shore bit, and Eddie jerked her alongside like a wild mare in a coral. We had made it to Panama.

22

I went immediately to the Navy office in Panama to report our arrival. I remembered the wide streets and the bazaars tucked in under overhanging porticoes and permanent tin awnings. There is a lot of rainy weather in Panama. There was something seedy about the town. The United States maintained the Canal Zone and tolerated the town. The impermanence of the arrangement was obvious. It was as if we felt that someday there would be an easier way of getting from ocean to ocean and that Panama was destined to be dropped like a hot potato. There was every evidence of a temporary and uneasy arrangement. It was not a warm and welcome partnership.

The shops were all tourist traps and the natives were less than second-class citizens. There was little national pride, nothing but the air of a sullen acceptance on their part and on ours.

The arrival of the ST250 was duly acknowledged, and I reported that we had experienced considerable engine trouble and that the request to bring a compass up to Limón could now be facilitated with no resort to the Air Force.

Muhammad had come to the mountain without the benefit

of a compass. The Navy officer smiled when I explained our impatience. I saw a Navy WAVE pounding away on a typewriter, and I requested permission to have her type a letter for me.

The letter was addressed to Mr. Lewis Higgins at the Port of Embarkation in New Orleans. It read:

> Subject: Change of status.
> Reference: Virgilio Varga, second officer; Bernard L. K. Kidd, deck hand.
> I have found it expedient and necessary to change the status of Virgilio Varga from second officer to that of deck hand and the status of Bernard L. K. Kidd from deck hand to second officer.
> You will kindly change all records to coincide.
> Respectfully,
> Joseph W. Richards,
> master of the U.S. Army ST250

I signed the letter, and it went off air mail within the hour. Then I returned to the tugboat. I was going to have to break the news to Virgilio.

I called him up on the boat deck. "Virgilio," I said, "I wonder if you have any idea about what the war that the United States is waging is all about."

Virgilio looked at me suspiciously. Virgilio was a complicated guy. He had grown up in Puerto Rico, and the philosophy of our system of government must have seemed to him to be an altruistic cover for corporate advantage. It was a kind of a game not too different from the Falangist notions that were common in Spanish countries.

I embarked on a hopeless and extraneous lecture on the democratic system. Virgilio waited. When I came to the part about a man's right to the rewards of his efforts, Virgilio glowered at me.

"Kidd," I said, "has learned to navigate. That is the job of

147

an officer. Kidd has become very valuable to me. I am going to promote him to the position of second officer."

"You are trying to put a knife in my back," said Virgilio.

"If you are worried about being abandoned in a foreign port, forget it," I said.

"You are trying to put a knife in my back," said Virgilio.

"Anyway you are now a deck hand," I said. I didn't go into the business about the heaving lines that he had swapped for booze or the hams that W. D. told me were missing from the freezer. I was not conducting a trial. Varga was a boozer. I had simply changed his status. I walked away.

Virgilio went below. There was no further trouble from him and damn little advantage in his services. I went back about my business.

The Army people brought our mail aboard. There was no mail for me, and what seemed even worse, not so much as a postcard from that living statue that was Ricky's wife. Ricky walked away from the mail call with tears in his eyes. It was painful.

Some engineers from the Canal Zone came aboard, and the mechanism that reversed the engine was repaired. We took on a pilot and proceeded into the locks and along the endless lake to Balboa, shaking like a leaf all the way.

There is a vast drydock resembling a tremendous pit scooped out of the ground in Balboa that can accommodate the greatest ships. When the tide went out and the gates were closed, the ST250 lay there lonely as a bean in a great tureen.

The engineers monkeyed with the engine, jacking her this way and that, and after several days they had her lined up. The gates were opened, the sea came in and we were afloat.

The engine ran quietly with no vibration. Buster wagged his tail in heartfelt appreciation. They brought us a new compass. We took on stores and got ready to leave in the morning.

We lay all night beyond the massive gate that kept the ponderous fresh-water lake from smashing down and rolling us keel over truck in an angry passion to seek the level of the sea.

We shoved off early into the Gulf of Panama. The great bight on the south side of the canal forces all ships whose destination is to the north to run south for a hundred miles before they can resume a northerly direction. The turning point is at Cape Mala, whose jutting promontory was a welcome sight in the heat of late afternoon. Even then it was southwest until darkness and then west until near daybreak.

We were down in a latitude of seven degrees, or less than five hundred miles from the equator. It was hot, and the wind coming off the land carried the fragrance of tropical vegetation. We picked up the light on the Island of Jicarón around midnight and for the first time since we had departed from Balboa we turned slightly north.

The heat of the tropical latitude stayed with us all night, but the knowledge that we were heading west-by-north was a cooling thought. Punta Burica was off the starboard bow in the morning.

Virgilio Varga had accepted his demotion, and although he was not happy about it, he no longer muttered about a knife in his back. At the noonday meal suddenly there was an elephant on the galley table. Ricky had assembled it from a couple of potatoes, some leaves of cabbage for ears, legs made of parsnips, and a big carrot for a trunk, all put together with toothpicks.

The indented coast line fell away, and we sighted Cape Blanco of Costa Rica and ran along the dramatic coast with its great cliffs of volcanic rock and a sparkling surf that curled along a sandy beach. We turned further to the north, skirting the coast of El Salvador, and late in the afternoon we came to the unprotected port of Champerico which is Guatemala's only access to the sea.

149

If necessity is the mother of invention, Champerico had both necessity and invention. There is no harbor, no inlet, nothing to give succor to a ship on the west coast of Guatemala. The hard rocky shore has defied man's need for a breakwater or a buffer against the constant pounding of the sea.

In an act of desperation, some British engineers were hired, and they solved the problem of a port by anchoring huge buoys to which the ships were moored and by constructing a dock of steel pins and wires that allows the raging surf to pass without resistance.

The pier extended several hundred feet out into the surf. When we approached the port we were directed to tie up to one of the enormous black buoys that resembled the buoys I had seen many years before moored in the raging current of the Hooglie River in Calcutta.

Eddie climbed out on the buoy and made our bow line fast. We waited. There were some puffs of white steam coming out of a stack that extended out of the roof of the covered pier. After a few minutes a section of the roof opened and a crane was seen raised in the air.

With a fierce puffing of the steam engine on the dock, the crane was seen lifting a great longboat and lowering it alongside. Then the crane went back and came up with a chair with three men hanging on to it. The chair was decorated in traditional Guatemalan style. It had a tasseled awning to shield the occupants from the sun, and it was painted in a spectrum of bright colors and there was even a cushion on the seat.

There were a couple of men holding the boat against the huge swells that came in out of the sea, and when the chair came down to the level of the boat, they all jumped aboard, manned the long oars, and were out to the tug in a matter of minutes.

We were rowed ashore. When we arrived alongside the pier, the chair came down again, and we were lifted three at a time up into the air and down into the dock through the great hatch in the roof.

We passed by some huge logs that were lying on the dock and went up into town. The place was clean and neat and typically Guatemalan.

It was a short visit. The men were so astounded by the manner in which they were brought ashore that they forgot all about the bars and the girls. In any case, we did not relish a night moored to that buoy in the open sea. We hurried down to the pier after a short turn around the pretty town and waited to be wafted three at a time up and over and down into the longboat.

While I was awaiting my turn, I asked the dockmaster what kind of wood those logs were that were piled on the dock. Some of them were twenty feet long and more than two feet in diameter.

"Lignum vitae," he said. "On account of the submarines there have been no ships in here for months."

Lignum vitae is a priceless ingredient of shipbuilding. Peacock was looking at them. There was a fabulous amount of money in those logs. Our shipbuilding industries would have paid any price for them. There was no substitute for lignum vitae when it came to fashioning the huge drive-shaft bearings for the Liberty ships.

According to Peacock, the fibers of the wood absorbed the lubricating grease, and the bearings never wear out. They were in desperate need for that wood in the States and there were no ships to come and get it.

If I had the little cargo vessel that Captain Larry and I had taken to Panama, I would have picked up a couple of those logs, paid for them, and sold them in San Pedro. As far as the ST250 was concerned, we were top-heavy as it was and, as Virgilio Varga had suggested, I decided not to "fawk around" with a deckload of lumber.

We left the way we entered. We were rowed out to the tug, the chair was lowered away to pick up the men who had ferried us out, and then the crane dipped down to pick up the longboat.

As we cast loose from the buoy, the huge opening in the roof of the dock closed, and the sea continued to sweep ashore unobstructed and endless.

23

I can't remember where it was that I heard about the Bay of Tehuantepec. It wasn't Captain Erbe and it wasn't any of the other captains whom I had shepherded to a safe landfall. It might have been some sailor in a bar describing the strange jeopardy of that area.

Kidd was at the helm as we took off along the coast of Guatemala at night. The sea was unobstructed by reefs or islands or shoals. The mountains or foothills of the Sierras came down abruptly into the Gulf of Tehuantepec. We ran in the lee of the highlands.

"Kidd," I said, "they tell me that it blows to seaward so hard that a ship was known to have battled the wind for three days trying to make port in the Gulf of Tehuantepec. It had to give up."

"What did they do?"

"They had to swing out wide and creep along the shore to avoid the ferocity of the wind."

"Is that what we are going to have to do?"

"I guess we'll have to hug the shore unless we want to be blown right out to sea."

"It could be murder in this trap," said Kidd.

Toward midnight we edged her in so close that the hills seemed to hang over us, and part of the sky was obscured by the mountains. At the first light of day, we came within a few hundred yards of the shore, and we began to feel the pressure of the wind striking us abeam on the starboard side.

By the time we got to the entrance of the harbor it was expedient to move in even closer to avoid being capsized.

The hundred yards that separated us from the land were still wide enough for the wind to generate a sharp and violent sea. It must have been hell offshore.

The ST250 managed to slug it out to the sea buoy and the harbor entrance. We ran the concrete-lined channel and entered the great square basin with its tin warehouses and English derricks all pointed to leeward like giant sea birds on the dock. There was only one other ship in the basin.

I walked along the pier. The vast tin warehouses were empty, and the rusty doors were hammering themselves into junk flapping in the constant moaning flow of air.

The other ship in the basin was a Mexican freighter that had sustained a gunshot hole forward and was only kept from sinking by flooding her afterhold so that she lay down by the stern. There was no one in sight anywhere. It was the equivalent of a ghost town on the sea. I had never come across anything like it. It is known as the Port of Salina Cruz.

We piled off the ship and went up into the town of Tehuantepec. We passed a government weather station on the way. There was a man on duty.

Ricky asked him in Spanish whether it blew like this all the time.

"Nine months of the year," he said.

I got Ricky to ask him about the harbor.

"It was built by the English just after the French gave up on the Panama Canal. They had an idea about transporting cargo destined for the Pacific over the pass between the mountains from Vera Cruz, which is just opposite Salina Cruz on the Gulf of Mexico."

"And we put them out of business by building the canal," I ventured.

"Si," said the man in the weather station. "They even had a plan to lift a ship right over the mountains through the pass on four sets of railroad tracks. It has all been forgotten. Life moves on. Salina Cruz is an orphan child. An orphan child that cost the British five million dollars."

Ricky translated most of this. It was tragic and it was funny. We walked along the road to the town of Tehuantepec, and suddenly there was not even the whisper of a wind. We had passed beneath that fierce layer of air that tunnels through the pass and is a terror to ships on the Gulf of Tehuantepec.

Ricky found a kind of a boarding-house restaurant, and we had an elegant meal in traditional Mexican style.

It was a nice vacation from the galley for W. D. and for Namb. Peacock drank too much tequila and we had to carry him back aboard the tug. He was the only one who got a good night's sleep. The rest of us were kept awake by the constant moaning of the wind and the banging of the loose tin on the warehouses that lined the basin.

Restless, I went back into Tehuantepec for a final look at the little town that lies at the base of a mountain.

Walking in the darkness, I experienced the same transition from the constant scream and moan of the wind in Salina Cruz to the blessed silence and calm of Tehuantepec.

There is a public park in the center of this clean little town. The park benches were brightly painted and arranged in a square with a carefully tended formal garden of flowers in the center. I sat on a bench under the soft street lights that competed with a sliver of moon. I was very tired.

It had been a long voyage in an impossible vessel. In the best of circumstances with an able and seaworthy ship, it would have been a difficult passage for a man with a hernia. I remembered my grandfather and the enormous burdens that he was able to carry despite a similar handicap. The hills

155

that rose above me to the south reminded me of a garden that he had built at the age of seventy, moving huge boulders up the hill to support the terraces.

Past the lights of the park there was a glow of warm light from the stained-glass window of a cathedral built by the Spanish halfway up the mountain. I thought about the effort, the dedication, the passion to complete the job demonstrated by the early settlers, and I realized that I was feeling sorry for myself.

I went back aboard the tug and fell asleep to the tune of a maelstrom.

24

It is just under three hundred nautical miles from Salina Cruz to Acapulco. The best we could do was nine knots. With a fair wind and a lucky current we could make it in thirty hours. We shoved off before the sun came up over the mountains and all morning we sneaked along the coast as close as we dared until the wind no longer threatened to toss us out to sea.

When we were out of the torrent of air that pours through the pass in the mountains, we directed our course a couple of miles off shore.

Now it was an easy passage in the lee of the mountain range. The engine was clicking off its revolutions at a steady pace. In the vicinity of Puerto Angel, after following a south-westerly course, we resumed a northwesterly direction close along the coast. I could see the surf creating a tenuous line of white against the dun-colored hills and the morning sun glancing off the shiny wet surface of the beach.

Ricky was off watch in the afternoon and he came up on the boatdeck. He was in the dumps about not having heard from Judy, his wife. We talked about his life in New Orleans, the sculpture he had done, the people he had known—mostly the girls. Ricky Alferez was a household word in New Orleans.

If this passage was instrumental in breaking up his marriage, I had the burden of guilt. I had offered him the job of oiler.

"Ricky," I said, "If you want to split in Acapulco, I will advance you the money to fly back to New Orleans."

Ricky shook his head no. "If you want to take off for New Orleans when we get to California, I can ship another oiler."

"No way," said Ricky. He was a die-hard.

It was a fair passage. The moon came up fatter and the stars were stitched all over the sky. I leaned out of the pilothouse window and tried to figure out whether I was lucky or damned. To have made this voyage in my own vessel would have been astronomically expensive. It would have taken four lifetimes to amass the wherewithal. Was I going to have to pay for it with my life?

My reverie was interrupted by W. D. who brought a pot of coffee and a couple of sandwiches up to the pilothouse. He stayed to watch the school of porpoises that were drawn to the turbulence of the bow and were diving, darting, leaving long silver wakes in the phosphorescent water.

We stood there, side by side at the open window of the pilothouse for the better part of an hour savoring the incidental advantages of a war. The dolphins took off for another watery playground and W. D. said goodnight and went below. The stars stayed with me until midnight when Eddie took over.

"Eddie," I said, as he took the wheel, "I wonder where in hell Dyer is with the ST249?"

"He ought to be in Wilmington, California by now. He had a five-day start."

"You can't win 'em all," I said, "Keep her on 281."

I hit the sack.

In mid-morning we came through the main channel into the expansive harbor of Acapulco. There is another narrow channel to the north of it, the one where they dive off the rocky cliff. We tied up along the concrete wall that lined the northern edge of the harbor.

The sky was a cloudless blue, and the primitive little town sported one small hotel with a bar, a marketplace, and a scattering of modest houses and shacks. Acapulco was bogged down by the war and basking in the charm of isolation. We ranged through the bazaars, the tourist shops, and the multicolored marketplaces. The day went quickly.

We moved the tug over to the oil dock and filled her bunkers. We came back and tied up close to town and near the only hotel. In the evening we all piled ashore and gathered around a table in the hotel restaurant. We ordered beer.

Ricky began to drink. It was the first time since we left New Orleans that he hit the bottle.

Ricky, for all his Spanish and Mexican heritage, was an Indian. Indians have never mastered the art of making booze or holding it. Ricky was no exception. After a couple of beers Ricky became talkative. He held center stage and he was fun to listen to. After four beers he began to grow sullen.

The waiter who brought us our drinks pointed out the mayor of Acapulco, who was having dinner at the table across the room. The mayor had a guest, a rangy-looking character with a goatee, an elaborate silver-embroidered jacket, and a fancy sombrero. He had on a pair of Mexican pants with all kinds of needlework, and he was sporting expensive cowboy boots with spurs.

Ricky knew the guy. He had been a great favorite of a president of Mexico whom Ricky had fought against in the revolution. Ricky stared at him and seethed.

I went to the head. When I came back out there was a resounding crash. Ricky had picked up the hombre by the waist and dumped him right on the mayor of Acapulco's dinner table.

The table was overturned. The enchiladas and the tortillas

went over with the china, the silver, and the glass. The mayor of Acapulco grabbed the bottle of wine by the neck and stood up. I extricated Ricky.

I sent him out into the night. Then I went back to apologize to the mayor and tried to get him to accept a bottle of wine in compensation.

He thanked me for the offer of wine and turned it down. He took my apology under advisement. We left the hotel soon after Ricky. I went up the hill and found a cute *muchacha* standing in a doorway, waiting for me.

We went into the little adobe house together.

Eddie woke me early. "Captain," he said, "the American consul is down in the galley. He wants to talk with you."

While I was getting dressed, Eddie filled me in. "After Ricky left the hotel last night he ran into a bunch of soldiers, and he started taking their rifles away from them. He had four when they called out the garrison. They have him locked up in the calaboose."

I came down the ladder and met the consul. He was very sympathetic. "There will be a trial this morning. I will go and speak for him," he said.

The trial was held in the city hall. The mayor of Acapulco presided. It looked bad for Ricky. They brought him into the courtroom in manacles. He was quite subdued.

The charge was read in Spanish and the consul translated. Ricky was accused of disturbing the peace and resisting arrest.

Whispering to the consul, I asked him to tell the mayor that Ricky was part of the United States Merchant Marine, which was fighting for democracy. The consul repeated my statement to the mayor.

The mayor replied in Spanish. The consul repeated his answer in English. "That is no reason for turning Acapulco into occupied territory."

I had to buy that. Nonetheless, it seemed to me that to an Indian, everything on this continent was occupied territory.

Sentence was pronounced. Ricky was fined five hundred pesos, or one hundred dollars.

I explained through the consul that I only had eighty dollars. The fine was reduced to four hundred pesos, and I walked out of there with Ricky.

We walked back to the tug. Ricky, chastened, walked behind us. The crew passed a hat around, and I got sixty dollars of the money back; I didn't care about the twenty I had lost. That is what Ricky's ancestors got for my hometown.

Ricky stayed below. He was abashed. Texas, the second enigneer, came up to the pilothouse to speak for him. "Captain," he said, "Ricky thinks that we had better get out of here. He is afraid that he killed a man last night at the jail."

"Now what in the hell did he do that for?"

"It was a trustee, one of the prisoners. He was beating Ricky with a bullwhip. You ought to take a look at his back. It is covered with bloody welts. Ricky hit him on the head with a rock and dragged him unconscious into the bushes in the prison yard."

I unhooked the speaking tube and whistled for Peacock. "Have you got any air in the tank?"

"Some," said Peacock.

"Get the engine going. We are getting out of here."

The engine coughed into life. Eddie let the lines go. We made a fast turn and headed for the open sea.

In case there was a government gunboat patrolling the main channel, we headed for the narrow one to the north. I broke out the chart of the harbor and rang the telegraph to "full ahead."

The great rock cliffs between which the channel passes loomed ahead. Peacock knew about the situation and had the engine wide open. We were really moving, when suddenly dead ahead of us a great black rock appeared, half awash and in the middle of the channel. I jumped on the telegraph and rang "full astern."

We backed in a great apron of foam. I took a fast gander at the chart. "There is no goddamn rock like that in the channel!"

But there it was, shiny and mean-looking, like a great cap of black volcanic rock polished by the sea. Before I could figure a way to get around it, a tremendous burst of water

and mist spouted from the blowhole in the rock. The head of the whale submerged and two enormous flukes big as hanger doors rose in the air before us.

Eddie was on the forepeak making up the lines. "Thar she blows!" he sang out. He jumped up behind the pilothouse to fetch a harpoon that Peacock had fashioned. We unlimbered a huge drum of emergency line that was carried for a breeches buoy. We forgot all about Ricky. We forgot all about jails and gunboats. We chased that whale out of the harbor and back into it again.

We chased a whale that sounded, rose to blow, and sounded again, changing course every time we saw him surface. We chased him for miles up the coast. We concentrated on the whale.

So did Ricky. He was out on the bow like a bronze statue of an Indian warrior armed with that homemade harpoon.

We never did harpoon that whale. It was just as lucky for us as it was for the whale. He could have turned us over with one flip of that gigantic fluke.

Something did happen, however, that made me wonder if a whaling vessel in the vicinity of Acapulco had not been successful in killing a mama whale.

We were proceeding in a northwesterly direction when Buster, back on the port quarter, began to bark. I walked back on the boat deck to find out what was getting him so excited. Coming alongside of our port quarter and rubbing its flank along our rubstrake was a baby whale evidently trying to suckle on the bilge of the ST250.

It came up to the tug repeatedly, and every time it did, Buster went into a spell of frenzied barking. Peacock came out of the engine-room door as the baby whale made another pass at the vessel. He ducked back behind the deckhouse and came to the port quarter with his homemade harpoon, just as Ricky, who had been taking a nap, came out of his cabin.

As the baby whale whirled about and made another pass— in the misguided notion that he could get some whale milk from the top-heavy tug—Peacock, armed with that lethal long spear, lifted his muscular arm for the kill.

It happened like greased lightning. Ricky came up beside Peacock just as the baby whale was nuzzling along the chine searching for the underwater teat. He took that spear away from Peacock just as easily as taking a lollipop away from a baby.

The baby whale, finding nothing but an iron belly covered with bottom paint and sea grass, took off in search of its mother or a more likely substitute.

Peacock and Ricky faced each other after Ricky put the harpoon away behind the electric windlass on the after deck. Peacock said, "You goddamn spick."

Ricky smiled. "You know, Peacock, you and I are going to have a fight."

Peacock glared at Ricky.

Ricky continued. "Yes, you and I are going to have a fight, and do you know, I am going to kill you. Do you know why?"

Peacock waited for the reason, frothing at the mouth.

"Because," said Ricky, "you are afraid to die and I am not." Ricky went back into his cabin and resumed his nap.

Now I knew how Ricky had taken four carbines away from the Mexican National Guard.

We kept on churning up the west coast of Mexico. I decided to make a run for it, all the way up to California. We had had enough goings on in Latin American ports, enough drinking and enough confrontations. Our business was getting the ST250 up to Wilmington, California and across to Honolulu.

I called the crew to the pilothouse and I told them what to expect. "It is going to be a long run, and the next time you set foot on a dock it will be in California."

25

By the time the baby whale got away it was evening and we were abreast of Punto Mangrove. The crew was somewhat subdued after that explosive evening in Acapulco, and whatever resentments had developed due to the booze and the feel of terra firma after the long tension on the tug was being rolled out of them in the easy gyrations of the ST250.

The crew had gotten so used to the danger of an imminent capsize that they took it in their stride. When she rolled way over and they were on the down side they no longer expected her to go all the way over. With that curious kind of faith, which was the only faith they knew, they simply waited for the vessel to right itself. There was no recourse to genuflection and no sudden prayer for salvation.

A pious sailor would have been so busy praying that he wouldn't be worth the powder to blow him to hell. By dawn we were off Punta San Telmo and heading for the Gulf of California.

We lost sight of the foothills of the Sierras, and we had to forgo the comforting realization of land on the starboard side as we entered the 260-mile mouth of the gulf.

Now it was night. The Gulf of California is alive with fish.

We watched the phosphorescent wakes of submarine life as the ST250 wagged her way in the dark across the opening of this underwater game preserve. Near as I could tell, there were some awful big ones playing around off the beam.

In the morning we got a good look at one. It was a hammerhead shark, and it looked half as long as our vessel, with its great vicious jaw. It followed along on the starboard beam and took off when it realized that there was nothing palatable about the vessel except the crew.

By noon the wind, which was off the land, moderated and we were ploughing along in almost flat calm. Peacock, who seemed to have a voracious appetite for disaster, rigged a plank out of the engine room door, constructed a ski, fastened it with some quarter-inch line and was over the starboard side, water-skiing.

Ricky was sitting on the bulwark forward watching him, wondering if Peacock wasn't trying to save him the trouble of keeping his promise to send him to the afterworld.

As the captain of the vessel, I was responsible for the lives of these men. On the other hand, Peacock was the boss of his own department. Furthermore, we all needed Peacock because of his ability as an engineer.

While I was debating my options to order him out of jeopardy, the crazy bastard got a leg on the outrigger and came aboard. There were no other challengers and the outrigger was dismantled.

It was very quiet at lunch.

26

After twenty-eight hours of open water, we sighted Cabo San Lucas, the cape at the southern tip of Baja California. There were no more pyrotechnics from the crew as we proceeded in a northwesterly course along the peninsula. We ran close aboard the Island of Santa Margarita some 150 miles northwest of the cape, and we lost sight of land till we picked it up again at Punta San Pablo, 220 miles northwest of Santa Margarita.

There is another great open bight in the coast of Baja California. After we took our departure from Punta Eugenia, except for the low profile of some scattered islands, there was no sight of land until Punta San Antonio rose above the horizon.

Now we were steering more north than west, and the curious elation of channel fever had the crew on tenterhooks as we slugged out the final miles of the second leg of the long voyage.

We had only 180 miles to go before we would pass the latitude that is the dividing line between the northern border of Mexico and the southern border of our native land.

We were still below that line when Peacock, true to form,

broke out his trusty harpoon and commenced to vent his hostility on a school of playful dolphins that congregated off the bow, a happy and innocent delegation gathered to welcome us back to home waters.

"Peacock, you crazy son of a bitch, cut that out," I shouted down at him. "You are going to cause a disaster."

I might just as well have saved my breath. He turned and sneered at me defiantly and kept right on stabbing away at the porpoises, coming up with tiny chunks of white meat as they wiggled free from the harpoon.

Besides having sympathy for those innocent sea animals, I believed in the superstition that it is the worst kind of luck to wound or kill a dolphin.

Peacock got bored with his malicious pastime after a while and went down below. I never did understand ship's engineers; and the vendetta that has been going on between the deck gang and the black gang ever since the unfortunate demise of the tall ships suddenly seemed justified.

I lived to see the chief engineer get his comeuppance. It was months later on another voyage. I had shipped with Peacock again. Not because I liked him but because he was a damn good engineer.

It was in Cameron, Texas. We were taking an Army aircraft rescue vessel from Brownsville to New Orleans. In Cameron, Peacock went ashore with the black gang. He got drunk and went into a dance hall. He was dancing with a little girl. Suddenly he picked her up and dumped her on the floor. Then he looked around at the startled dancers and said, "Fuck you all!"

Back at the vessel, the boys told me, "The chief engineer is in jail."

"I am not surprised," I said. "He's a criminal." Then I got the story.

There happened to be a Texas Ranger in the dance hall. He was six foot six and built like a bulldozer. He walked over to where Peacock was leering at the crowd and pulled his gun. Then he proceeded to gun-whip him. The black gang didn't dare come to his rescue.

Then he handcuffed Peacock, shoved him out of the place, and threw him into the car. They drove off. Passing a place that was in Louisiana, Peacock growled that the officer was out of his jurisdiction and demanded to be released.

At that point the ranger took him out of the car and beat the living hell out of him. Then he threw him back into the car and took him to the slammer.

The last thing he said as they locked him up was, "He didn't knock me out."

He didn't knock him out, but when he paid the fine and he got back to the ship, I have never seen a man so unmercifully battered. His face was unrecognizable. It was swollen so badly and so disfigured that he did not even vaguely resemble homo sapiens. He looked like he had been through a meat grinder.

When we delivered the vessel to New Orleans, the report had come from Texas; Peacock was thrown out of the service. I never saw him again.

I hope the porpoises of Punta San Antonio are still smiling about it. Or, at least, still smiling.

We kept right on moving all that night. I was in the sack at about four o'clock in the morning when I felt the tug pitch violently. She took to rolling, canting over to a disastrous degree. Then she would pitch forward wildly and rise up to plunge again. I pulled on my pants and went out into the pilothouse. Virgilio was at the wheel and Eddie was struggling to take it away from him.

I said, "All right, I'll take the wheel."

They moved aside. The tug made another miserable dive into a massive wave that was topped with foam like the white knuckles of a giant fist. The tug shuddered and rolled with the punch. I rang the telegraph to slow her speed.

It was a tiny bit better now. The sea was monstrous. It took all the skill I had to counter every malicious wave that was bent on beating us down and turning us over.

The trick was to put her head directly into the wave and give her a short burst with the engine to keep her from going over.

I knew how to do it. I also had help from Peacock who was fast as lightning at the controls.

Every wave carried the threat of extinction. There was no one on board who could relieve me at the wheel. It was a wild time, and the men had a haunted look on their faces as they watched the fateful juggling act.

We were approaching Coronado Island. On account of the weather there was no possibility of ducking in there. We were going to have to keep right on going. I began to wonder if I had the stamina.

"Eddie," I said, "would you be good enough to fetch my truss? It is hanging at the foot of my bunk."

Eddie went back into the cabin, picked up my truss and brought it out to me. I thanked him and slipped the steel spring that held the pad in place around my waist right on top of my pants and adjusted the pad into place. Then I swung the wheel violently to port to counter a massive sea that hurled green water over the bow and smashed against the forward bulwark of the pilothouse.

I must have appeared as an odd-looking character at the wheel, with that shiny spring around my waist and the black pad holding my guts in place jammed in against my crotch. No one in the pilothouse laughed at me. They didn't even smile. We were skirting the edge of the hereafter and they knew it. Most of the crew who had been flooded out of their cabins were gathered around me in that tiny pilothouse. I glanced at their faces as wave after wave mounted its deadly assault. There wasn't a face that was not frozen in apprehension.

It went on for hours, each wave vying with the last to be

the one that would capsize the tug. We beat them all with that inadequate rudder backed up with that willing Enterprise engine. Peacock, for all his imbecility, was on the ball. Every time a gigantic wave rose on our port quarter and I rang the telegraph for "full ahead," there was an immediate response, and the vessel shook with the whining answer of the diesel.

It went on for hours. There was no respite. We inched forward careening down the after slope of every wave, only to be brought to a violent standstill as the next one presented another high wall of water.

The galley was flooded, and W. D. was up in the pilothouse with most of the deck gang. There would be no breakfast and no coffee to sustain us. As sea after sea carried on in that monotonous determination to drown us, I said, "How would you fellows like to give me a hand?"

There was a general nodding of heads in assent.

"You can help me and maybe save your own skins by climbing down through the fidley and keeping Peacock company. It must be lonely down there, and you know the chief, he likes an audience. He is doing as much to keep this trap from turning turtle as I am."

They got the pitch. One by one they braved the claustrophobia of the engine room to reduce the weight aloft. Soon, the first light of day gave me a better look at what was going on ahead.

Eddie stayed with me in the pilothouse. He was wise now to the rhythm of my method, and he rang the telegraph when I nodded my head and slowed her down as each crisis swept aft.

It was the same thing all that day. It was almost as bad all night. W. D. managed to duck into the galley at the risk of being grabbed by an erratic wave and dragged over the side. He came up with a pot of coffee and a bucket of leftover bread and meat. The coffee was cold, but it worked. We got a second wind and an angry determination to beat the odds.

171

I drifted into a kind of euphoria of fatigue. In a dreamy reflection as I countered every wave, I saw the sea as a vast impersonal thing, the sweet home of the playful dolphin, the all-pervading mattress and comforter of the thoughtful whale, the romping ground for all kinds of tricksters, bent on gobbling one another in a humorless round robin. A man had no business at sea, certainly not in a sea like this one and in a vessel that was itself a nightmare.

I thought of people whose whole lives flashed through their brains at the moment of death, and I tried to remember a particular time when being in a predicament like this would have seemed fantastic and utterly improbable: Like when I was painting pussy willows in PS 14 at the age of ten, or when I won a dozen tennis balls by beating some young braggard 6–love–6–love at a summer camp for boys in the Adirondacks, or the time I had Betsy Flemming out on a date in my Model T, and she cried like a baby because she wanted to do it so badly, and we didn't do it. Then we parted for a year, and when I saw her again, she had so many pimples that I didn't want to do it.

I thought about my grandfather, who had to have his leg amputated at the age of seventy-three, and how my mother told the doctor that grandpa would rather die than have his leg amputated; the doctor asked her what the hell she knew about what grandpa wanted.

I remembered breaking the news to grandpa. "It is either your leg or you."

I remembered his answer. "Cut it off," he said.

"Cut it off," I said.

"What did you say, Captain?" said Eddie.

"I'm sorry, Eddie, I was just thinking about what my grandfather said when I told him that they had to amputate his leg."

"I understand," said Eddie.

"Eddie," I said, "My dad has a droll sense of humor."

"What the hell is 'droll'?"

"Well let's say he has a sense of humor." I went on. "One time he sent me a postcard. He was staying at an oceanfront resort. There was a picture of a wave breaking on the beach. On the back of the card he wrote, 'I don't know what the ocean is so excited about.' "

Eddie smiled. "It sure is excited now." Just as he said it, a lesser wave tried to climb over the bow and failed. It was the beginning of the end of a full day and a full night of hell.

The wind shifted from the northwest and came around slightly to the east, and the change in its direction quickly cut down on the ferocity of the sea. Through the spume we caught the dim outline of Coronado Island. Soon we were under the lee of it, and the ocean was no longer so excited. W. D. came up with some hot coffee, and Peacock came up out of the recesses of the engine room on the outside ladder instead of crawling up through the fidley.

He stood there in the pilothouse with a sweaty bandanna tied around his bull neck. He was bushed and I was bushed.

"Peacock," I said, "You broke one of the ten commandments of the sea. I don't know what the rest of them are, but the one you broke is, 'Thou shalt not harpoon a porpoise.' "

Peacock stared ahead out of the pilothouse window. I hit him again. "You came near killing all of us."

I gave Kidd the wheel and a course to follow. Then I went aft and closed my cabin door. I fell asleep with the truss still outside my pants.

27

Less than a hundred miles to the northwest was the port of Wilmington, deep in the harbor of Los Angeles. With a speed of nine knots the ST250 could make it in a day. The storm that we had just weathered brought a torrent of rain, and the last hours of the second leg of the voyage gave us a prolonged sample of what is known in California as "liquid sunshine."

It rained for a solid month. We sighted the long breakwater at Long Beach in the afternoon. The rain came down so hard that it flattened the seas, and the top-heavy little tug ran through the long swells as if she had never heard of her tendency to turn over. We waited at the breakwater for a pilot, passed under the bridge at Seaside Avenue, and tied up in the basin at Wilmington in a downpour.

Strangely enough, our so-called friend and rival had not arrived. Our satisfaction at having beaten Dyer again was tempered by the sobering realization that the ST249 might have capsized and gone down.

I reported our arrival to the Army people and waited for orders to proceed to Honolulu. I had put in a hitch in the Marine Corps, and I knew that a war was mostly waiting.

This wait in the rain for damn near a solid month was the most exasperating, morale-eroding wait I have ever known.

Sometimes, in the long dreary interval while the rain came down in buckets, I wondered if some reasonable character in the top echelon of Army brass had developed a measure of sanity and had decided not to allow the ST250 to expose herself to the periodic violence of the Pacific.

The prospect of twenty-four hundred miles of ocean before the job of delivering the ST250 to Honolulu was completed, together with the mystery of what happened to the ST249, began to have its effect on the crew.

There were diversions despite the rain. We collected our pay and we walked along the asphalt boardwalk at Long Beach, with the rain sweeping across the row of amusement places in a gale of wind. I even took a bus and went up to Hollywood just to get away from the scene. It was too wet up there for man or make-believe, and I dragged myself back to the tug, wet and bedraggled.

Eddie was in the pilothouse when I got back. "Captain," he said, "some of the crew want to talk to you."

"What do they want?"

"I guess you will have to ask them."

"Send them up."

Eddie climbed down the ladder and came back up with Virgilio Varga right behind him. Varga stood there glowering.

"What can I do for you, Virgilio?"

"You can pay me off," he said, "that's what you can do."

"How the hell can I pay you off?"

"Just write a letter, and I will take it over to the Army office."

"Look, Virgilio," I said, "did you ever hear of the War Manpower Act?"

"Captain, I am thirty-eight years old now. I am not worried about the draft anymore."

I looked at Virgilio and thought about it. He had an angle.

He also had a haunted look in his eyes. The Pacific Ocean lay out there to the west, and Varga wanted no part of it.

"Besides," said Virgilio, "I do not feel well and I am tired of going to sea."

There was an awesome pause. Then Eddie piped up, "Go ahead and write the letter, Captain, put down 'reason for discharge, sick and tired.' "

"O.K.," said Virgilio with a kind of a wry smile on his face.

I wrote the letter just like Eddie dictated. Under reasons for discharge I wrote, "Sick and tired."

Just as I signed the request Namb appeared in the pilothouse.

Eddie said, "Namb wants to pay off too."

Namb stood there peering through his cheaters. "Now don't tell me that you have just had your thirty-eighth birthday."

"No," said Namb.

"Then what-the-hell kind of a reason can I give for you to pay off?"

"I want to pay off," said Namb.

"Do you know what they are going to do to you after you pay off?"

Namb had no idea.

"They are going to throw your ass in the army. That's what they are going to do. Now what kind of a reason can I give for paying you off except to say that you have rocks in your head. You don't want me to say that you are crazy, do you?"

"Yes," said Namb, "that's fine."

I was only too happy to oblige. I was not at all sorry to see the last of them. Tony, the deckhand who was on Eddie's watch, paid off as well. When Varga came back from the army office to pick up his gear, I asked him what happened when the colonel saw the reason for his discharge.

Varga hesitated for a moment. Then he repeated the colonel's words, "Hell," said the colonel, "we are all sick and tired."

176

28

Buster never made it to Honolulu. I will never know whether he made it at all. During one of the rare times when it didn't rain, I decided to take Buster for a walk. I was standing on the main deck, and I saw Kidd up on the boat deck.

"Hey, Kidd," I called to him, "will you hand Buster down for me?"

"Sure," said Kidd. He went back in the pilothouse and dragged Buster out by the collar. Then he lifted him up, and before I could get under him, Kidd let him go.

Buster landed on the steel plate of the main deck on his side. He was never the same. Maybe he had a touch of distemper from the long rainy season and the violence of the passage. The fall didn't help any. Before I could get him to a vet, Buster got the running fits. He took off in the direction of Hollywood to join the expanding contingent of sick and erratic personalities.

I missed Buster. He had been a good friend. Thinking about our chances of making it across the Pacific, I was just as glad that we were spared the sin of leading Buster to his doom.

After a couple of weeks of wet boredom, we received

orders to take the ST250 down to Newport Beach. She was going into drydock for extensive changes. The Army evidently had an idea.

The idea was even worse than the original concept. They were determined to make her more top-heavy than ever.

When we got down to Newport Beach, they hauled her out of the water and got to work. They fashioned an enormous platform of yellow pine and fastened it down on top of the pilothouse. Then they mounted two fifty-caliber machine guns on top of the platform.

Not content with the certainty of disaster that they were preparing for us, the enterprising boondogglers proceeded to fasten two enormous ammunition cases behind the guns up on that platform.

I couldn't believe it. I watched the operation in a kind of startled trance. For the ST250, two 50-caliber machine guns were patently idiotic. A submarine could stand off at five miles and blow us to hell-and-gone with a five-inch gun and armor-piercing fragmentation shells. I walked up to the foreman in charge of this latest demonstration of lunacy.

"What in God's name is the idea of mounting that heavy platform and those two machine guns, to say nothing of the ammunition boxes, on top of my tug?"

His answer was an example of the kind of reasoning that could have lost the war for us. He said, "Morale purposes."

"Look, you crazy son of a bitch. That tug is top-heavy as it is. Furthermore, we are not going to challenge any Jap submarine to a duel."

"Orders is orders," he said. He looked at me as if he wanted to fight. I wish he had tried. I was ready to beat the hell out of him.

I walked out of the drydock with Eddie, and we had a couple of boilermakers and a beer chaser. "Eddie," I said, "we've got a problem."

"What's that?" said Eddie.

"Do you know what a cold chisel is, and a maul?"

"I sure do."

I bought another round. "Eddie, I know that you have a positive genius for acquiring certain government properties. Like the time you managed to latch onto that kedge anchor."

Eddie nodded sagely.

"This time it isn't government property that we need. The stuff belongs to the shipyard. See if you can borrow a couple of mauls and some cold chisels. We will kind of forget to return them. Just lose them down in the lazarette. Make sure the chisels are sharp."

"They'll be sharp." Eddie lifted his drink. "Don't worry about that."

"While you are at it, a couple of wrecking bars will come in handy, you know, the big ones."

"I read you, Captain," said Eddie.

A couple of nice-looking heads came in the bar. They were amiable and receptive and I bought them drinks. We continued our discussion about the tug. The girls wanted to know what it was all about.

"It's a military secret," I said.

"That's right," said Eddie, "did you ever amfsgay at the degus. You know, down by the L and N."

The girls looked puzzled. Eddie was exercising a twaddle at which he had become proficient. It was composed of real words, make-believe words, pig latin, expletives, and whatall. He could go on for hours without making a damn bit of sense. It would send me into gales of laughter. I had heard him practice it on drunks and foreigners. There was always an ingratiating smile on his face when he went into that routine. The people he practiced it on would always agree, sometimes in Spanish and sometimes in a kind of friendly drunken spirit of good will. Eddie was always better at it when he was half-crocked. One of the girls thought he was cute. The other one was convinced that Eddie was putting her on. She got up and walked out of the place. I got up and took her home.

We stopped at the shipyard on the way. It was dark, and the tug was silhouetted against the stormy sky, with her two machine guns pointing at some imaginary enemy. It started to rain. We went up the ladder to my cabin.

Her name escapes me. Her kiss did not. We crawled into my bunk, where for weeks and weeks I had sweated out an agony of apprehension. Now that the ST250 was solidly on chocks with no danger of a sudden capsize, I finally understood what had been missing.

Now the rolling and the rocking and the gyrations of desire mounted into a heavenly variation on a theme that had been unmitigated agony. It was a stormy sea and a violent crescendo, and as the waves receded, we fell into a timeless sleep.

I took her home through the drizzle at dawn.

29

Having rediscovered the missing element in my life, I pursued it with a vengeance. 1944 was a time in the lives of a lot of Americans when the advisability of an impermanent arrangement was axiomatic. Nobody bugged you to get married.

It had been a long war, and the efforts made to remain continent were beginning to fall apart. Booze was the catalyst. Booze and the realization that the boys were undoubtedly whooping it up over there.

Ricky was suffering. He hadn't had a word from Judy. I didn't understand why he insisted on hanging around until we made it to Honolulu, or didn't. I bled for him and for Buster, whose affection for me was total and heartrending.

I made a special trip to Wilmington to look for the dog, with no success. Meanwhile, they kept on fastening that useless junk to the pilothouse of the ST250. I had a strange awareness of doom. I found tranquility in the barroom.

The sense of doom was endemic. One gal who couldn't wait till her man came home nevertheless dreaded the day. I knew that it was on her mind. She hadn't said a word about a husband overseas, but at the climactic moment she grabbed me in a consuming passion, and cried, "Daddy, daddy, daddy."

She didn't mean me. I couldn't take it. I never went back, and she never came looking for me.

There were so many amateurs around that the professionals must have been starving. I met a couple of girls in a bar who showed an overweening interest in me. I had a couple of drinks, but I was far from crocked.

They evidently had been lapping it up. They figured that I was drunk, and they decided to take me home with them and put me to bed.

They bundled me into a cab. One was a middle-aged gal whom Eddie would have described as a "spook." The other one was young, stacked, and very decorative. When they got me into their apartment they started to undress me and put me in bed. I fought them off. I was embarrassed about the truss.

I undressed in the bathroom, and rolled up the truss in my pants. Then I joined them in bed. I didn't get to first base.

I have since been exposed to the wisdom of Samuel Pepys. He described a meeting in the park with two women whom he had "in order of their seniority."

Back on the tug in the morning, I got a message from the colonel in charge of Military Intelligence.

Eddie gave me the message. The colonel in charge of Military Intelligence had an office over in Wilmington. I was having a cup of coffee in the galley when Eddie handed me the note. It meant that I had to hop on a bus and travel twenty-odd miles back to Wilmington.

It worried me. Eddie was standing there with one foot up on the swivel chair stirring his coffee. "What in hell do you suppose he wants?" I said.

Eddie shrugged. "You haven't been giving away any military secrets, have you?"

"Maybe," I said, "you never know."

We had been so involved with our private war with the sea

that we had lost track of World War II. This wild wet holiday in California had taken me into a lot of swinging places. I had met a raft of unconventional people. Who knows, maybe I had shot off my big mouth.

I went over to Wilmington to find out. I walked into the office of Military Intelligence. There were a dozen gals at desks pounding away on typewriters. I asked the receptionist for the colonel.

She said, "He is out right now. I expect him back in about an hour. Won't you have a seat?"

I sat there in the big room with the clatter of typewriters all around me, and I thought about the boy friends and the husbands of these gals clattering away with machine guns on a Pacific island. Modern warfare was an affair of machines. For my war with the sea, I was equipped with the sorriest kind of machine, and the Army was busy making it worse.

I sat there trying to remember what I had said, what vital information I had blabbed that could have rated this call from Military Intelligence. The invitation was casual enough. They hadn't sent the Military Police to pick me up. It would have been less trouble if they had.

In any case, the worst that they could do was to slap me in the slammer for shooting my mouth off. I remembered talking to an old shellback who was weaving one of those enormous rope bumpers called puddings, which grace the bow of most tugboats. He had a full-rigged white beard, and he worked with the rope and the fid with a skill that reminded me of a sailor who said, "Those old-timers could weave a peacock on a cork fender."

"Pardon, me, pop," I said, as he kept right on following the fid with the line, "Did you ever make the run out to Hawaii in a sailing vessel?"

He stopped for a moment to light his pipe. "Sure did," he said.

"Could you give me an idea about how you did it. Did you run right out of here and follow the great circle?"

"Hell no," he said. "We sailed south for better than a couple hundred miles. Picked up a favorable current and a fair wind down around the island of Guadalupe. It took us right across." The old man went back to his chore, puffing away on his pipe and pounding the stubborn sisal cable down into place with a wooden mallet. I left him there practicing his archaic art. A shaft of light was coming through the great open door of the shed, illuminating the old man and his masterpiece.

I could not for the life of me recall having tipped off anyone else about our projected voyage. Certainly that old man was no informer.

I got bored worrying about it and fell asleep. I had come to the conclusion that a jail term, at least for the duration, was far better than a fatal capsize in the Pacific.

When I woke, all the girls were laughing. I must have been snoring. The colonel showed up after a while, swung into his office, and took me along.

"I understand that you are the captain of the ST250." I owned up. He studied me for a minute. "We are putting a couple of men aboard your vessel."

"That's fine," I said, "we're shorthanded."

"One of the men that we are putting aboard has been under surveillance."

"Under what?"

"He may be a spy." I could feel my jaw sag.

"What did he do?"

"Nothing that we know." said the colonel. "We thought it advisable to let you know. You will keep this information confidential."

"Sure, sure," I said. "Which one is the spy?"

"Fieffer," he said.

I was glad to get out of there. All my fears about giving away military secrets were unfounded. It did seem fantastic, however, that on top of all our other problems we should be saddled with a spy.

When I got back to the tug I found that the ST249, which had taken her departure from Panama five days before we left, had finally showed up. She was being hauled out in Newport Beach and the shipyard gang was fixing to load her pilothouse with the yellow pine platform, the machine guns, and the ammunition cases, in the same idiotic pattern as the ST250.

I paid it no mind. Eddie and I had our own plans for survival. After the bottom was painted, we slid back into the water and our bunkers were filled. A few days later, we left Newport Beach and ran back to Wilmington in consort with the ST249. It was a dead heat.

Waiting for the final orders to take our departure for Honolulu, Peacock invited me down into the engine room and showed me a hole in the hull as big around as a half dollar. The sea was pouring in. The hole was near the waterline, where some careless shipyard worker had somehow rested his aceteline torch. We careened the tug with a cable from the boat deck to the dock, and the damage was repaired. It was the only time when the tender characteristics of the vessel—her ability to lean over—came in handy.

The two new deck hands showed up. One was a clean-cut looking, typical American boy. He came up the ladder to the pilothouse with an omelet of gold braid on the visor of his cap. If it wasn't for his cherubic face I would have taken him for a rear admiral. He was the fanciest-dressed deck hand I had ever laid eyes on. He was dressed in an immaculate blue uniform. The other fellow wore a singlet and dungarees. His name was Fieffer. He was the spy.

The stores were brought aboard, and I was presented with a .45-caliber Colt automatic and enough morphine to keep an addict high as a kite for months. We had everything we would have to have in an emergency except the most important thing of all. We had no chronometer to find our longitude. A couple of soldiers, one a private and the other a P.F.C., came aboard to man the machine guns.

There was another long delay waiting for orders to sail. The wind from the northwest and the periodic rain continued with monotonous persistance. A small high-octane gasoline tanker, like the one I had been mate on, headed out into the Pacific. They found the seas too monstrous, turned tail and ran back in. The captain of the tanker was scared. They fired him and installed a new skipper.

At last it was our turn. I had orders to leave at dawn. I grabbed several cartons of cigarettes from the PX and we shoved off. I didn't bother to wait for Dyer and the ST249.

We headed out to the breakwater that protects Los Angeles Harbor from the ferocity of the northwest gales. Passing through the opening, we breasted the seas that were climbing over the breakwater.

My orders were to follow the great circle course to Honolulu. We made a beeline for Avalon on the lee side of Catalina Island. It was six o'clock in the morning.

By nine o'clock we were under the lee of the island. It was comparatively calm. We had been rolling precipitously for three hours. I rang the telegraph to stop the engine and we drifted. Eddie broke out the sledge hammers, the cold chisels, and the wrecking bars, and we went to work. Fieffer, the spy, held the cold chisel and Eddie swung the maul. They cut loose the machine guns and the black gang carried them down below and stowed them in the engine room. Kidd pried loose the heavy pine platform and the whole crew helped tilt it over and launch it over the side. We tore loose the ammunition cases and stowed them down below. The soldiers were cooperative. I explained to them that it was just a temporary expedient and that we would replace the guns when the weather moderated.

With the redisposition of weight from the top of the pilothouse to the recesses of the engine room there was a discernable improvement in the balance of the vessel. Now we were ready to face the Pacific Ocean.

Even in the comparative calm under the lee of Catalina

Island, I noticed that the fancy deck hand began to get queasy. By the time we rounded Catalina and headed south-west, he was hanging over the boat deck rail retching in earnest. I thought he was going to die. He turned to the color of a plum. I have never seen a man retch so violently for such a protracted period and to such little avail.

The ST250 no sooner cleared the shelter of Catalina Island than she encountered the brunt of the hard northwest gale. The course was west-by-south, or 260 on the compass. The gobbledygook I had received from the Navy Office about hitting a series of positions in the great-circle course from Los Angeles to Honolulu was obviously impossible. There was no chronometer on board. I didn't bother to explain the situation to the man who handed me my orders. He was a Naval Reserve officer, and he knew as much about naviga-tion as W. D., the cook.

If I ran down the latitude of Honolulu we were bound to hit it on the nose. It is nice to have a chronometer to give you Greenwich time in order to calculate a longitude. You don't need one to ascertain your latitude at noon. The big problem was how to keep this cast-iron canoe on its feet. Standing at her helm, I felt like a West Indian laundress with the wet wash of the whole town balanced on my head.

Fieffer, the spy, who was on my watch, was standing next to me at the wheel talking a blue streak. He was the most voluble spy I had ever heard of. I had always thought of a spy as being taciturn and sinister. This guy was the most outgoing spy in the world.

As the force of the storm increased it looked like the ST250 would surely go over. Green water mounted the mea-ger forefoot of the tug and convulsed against the bulkhead of the pilothouse. I slowed the engine and kept right on quar-tering the mean grey seas. Fieffer was leaning against the binnacle, going on about how his family moved from Sacra-mento to Los Angeles, which was the reason why he never got to go to kindergarten.

There was something banging around behind the pilothouse. I sent Fieffer back on the boat deck with a length of line to put a lashing on it. When he got back I asked him how the rear admiral was doing.

"He is still seasick," said Fieffer, who then proceeded to relate how he graduated from a kiddy car to a scooter, from a scooter to a bicycle, and from a bicycle to a motor scooter.

The ferocity of the storm grew worse. The northwest winds and rain that had started way back a month ago, when we were approaching Coronado, had built up a stupendous sea. The waves towered above the little ship. I began to have serious doubts about the ability of the tug to survive. I looked at Fieffer. He kept right on yacking away about his early years, completely oblivious. I smiled, slowed her down, and kept on quartering the onslaught.

Fieffer was facing the port window of the pilothouse. "Captain," he said, "guess who is right out there on our beam?"

It was the ST249, with Dyer at the wheel, smashing into the wild and heaving water with its engine wide open.

"He is hell bent on beating us to Honolulu," I said, "I hope he doesn't end up in Fiddler's Green."

It went on like that all day. The ST249 was soon lost to sight in the sweeping veil of rain and spume. The cabins were flooded down below and the crew came up in the pilothouse. W. D. came up the ladder and announced that there was a foot of water in the galley. There would be no more chow until the sea moderated.

Around sundown we had run far out beyond San Clemente Island, and the prospect of darkness and a continuation of what we had faced all that day began to get to me.

Eddie was in the pilothouse. I could see the concern on his face. "It is no use, Eddie," I said, "I am going to turn her around. We won't go back into the harbor. We'll try to duck behind San Clemente and sweat out this storm in the lee."

While we talked, Ralph, the deck hand with the gold

braid, clutched the lee rail of the boat deck with his mouth open and his eyeballs coming out. The massive combers that raked across from the northwest were getting bigger. It was time to turn. Another half hour and it might be too late. It seemed too late already when I saw my chance. It was provided by two giant combers, which from the different ways they came at us, seemed likely each to cancel out the force of the other.

We were all set. The chief had dogged the engine room doors and the black gang was using the ventilator in the fidley for access. The crew had taken shelter down in the engine room. All that remained to be looked after was the rear admiral, who hung like an abandoned coat over the boat-deck rail. I hollered to the spy to grab him and rang the telegraph "full ahead."

The wheel went hard over. On a flat carpet of foam we faced about like a cadet. We had turned in less than our length.

I cut her speed immediately, and we drifted along like a stroller in a rushing crowd, with the combers passing and crashing before us.

In the respite from the onslaught we breathed easier, but in the darkness and the easy motion we were plunging toward the stone shoulder of the Sierras that drops abruptly into the sea. For the moment, at least, we relished the brief holiday from the constant pound and burst of brine.

Ricky came up out of the engine room. "Where are you going?" he asked.

"We're heading back."

"No, no," said Ricky.

"Don't worry about it. We're going to duck behind San Clemente Island until this storm lets up."

Ricky shrugged and went below. In the respite from the pitch and roll that put the galley doors under, the crew made a wild dash for food—all but the highly decorated deck hand, who was doing his level best to turn himself inside out.

189

I wondered what to do with him for the night. His cabin was flooded. The engine room with its fumes was no place for him. I had the spy lug him into my cabin and hoist him up into my bunk. The screen was removed from the port next to his head so that he could puke out of the port.

The intensity of the wind grew worse. I had only the haziest notion of our position. We kept looking for the lighthouse on San Clemente with no success. We had evidently gone further out than I calculated during the hours of daylight. I gave up trying to pick up the light on the island and began to edge her south.

It was a tricky balancing act. The tug was rolling wildly. I had to avoid the island now and edge her as far south as she would go without spilling her. Some of the crew, sensing the turbulence, came up out of the engine room and camped around the pilothouse, watching in silence. It was a long night.

Fieffer kept right on telling the story of his life in California. I could hear the moan of the man in my bunk, the rush of the spume in the dark and the whine of the wind in the signal halyards, all mixed up with the yak of the spy.

There was fear. Every time I tried to edge her away from the lee shore that seemed to loom in the blackness, the ornery pot would lay over and stay there. Her freeing ports were inadequate to the seas that collected on her deck. If I didn't ring the engine room telegraph "full ahead" and put the helm hard right to get her up on her feet, she would have surely gone over.

By the first light of day I thought I could see a kind of cat's fur on the backs of the big rollers that came from a new quarter. A change in the direction of the wind would cross up the sea and chop it down. I tried to discount the notion, but it persisted.

Suddenly I realized that it was true. We were beginning to run out of the storm. More and more I turned the vessel south and she took it standing up. The crisis had passed. The wind was cutting the combers down to size and the spy was up to the part where he ditched his motor scooter in favor of the opposite sex—and beer too—all at the Bund meetings.

By eight o'clock in the morning, when Eddie came on watch, the sea had moderated to a point where it would tolerate us in its trough. I put the little ship back on the course that added up to eight, chased the rear admiral out of my bunk, and fell asleep.

I dreamed about riding a Coney Island roller coaster non-stop to Honolulu. It was no dream. When I woke the wind was dead aft and blowing a full gale. The tug was riding the rollers full tilt with the combers breaking over her freeboard. Mountains of green water toppled us along, reaching out in surf that whiplashed the poop.

I asked Fieffer, the spy, to take the wheel. After a few minutes I could tell that he knew his business. He was good. I could see that whatever sleep I had coming in heavy weather would be thanks to him.

In the last eighteen hours we had come far enough south to find the edge of the westerly current. I remembered the old shell-back who was weaving a tugboat pudding. He was right. Like the square-rigged ships that sailed south to pick up a fair wind, we had found the proper course for Honolulu.

I put the Navy sailing directions away in the desk drawer of my cabin and forgot about them, just like Captain Erbe.

30

The miserable wet wind that had swept down from Siberia for so long was now deflected off the dry Sierras and robbed of its rain. It came at us clear and cool, and it blew with a sustained and mighty vigor. I could almost see the old tall ships bracing their yards and the old sail crackers ordering the topsail and the stunsails bent. We flew. At times we were moving at the rate of twelve knots.

The gold-braided deck hand, whose name was Ralph, was still aboard and still among the living, if you could call that living. He stood in plain view at the starboard rail of the boat deck well forward. It appeared from his color that he was reversable after all. No native of this planet could be that purple on the outside, but he was getting ready to turn. There was just a touch of green along the edges of his ears. It wasn't too bad against all that gold braid. It gave him a kind of tarnished, seagoing look.

Eddie was talking to him between heaves. He had his hand on his shoulder. When he came into the pilothouse I asked him how the rear admiral was doing.

"Not too good," said Eddie, "I told Ralph that when he

felt that hairy feeling in his throat, for God's sake, swallow. He asked me why."

"What did you tell him?"

"I told him that the hairy feeling was the hair on his ass, and if he didn't swallow, he would sure as hell turn himself inside out."

The sun was in the middle of the sky and the air was as clear to the eye as the western desert. I took a noon sight and then took the wheel from the spy. I wanted to save him for later so I could get some sleep. We were getting down to the latitude of Honolulu, but we had a long way to go. Our little radio was too far away now to pick up the time tick from Arlington. There was no way to figure a longitude or estimate when we would make a landfall.

The spy hung over the binnacle. He would rather talk than sleep. He was in rare form, going on about the big Bund meetings, the big times, the big-busted Fräuleins, the big steins of beer. Everything was big, even the arguments. It seems like Fieffer didn't agree.

"I was always fighting their screwy ideas. I had a lot of Jewish friends. I would have walked out of there, but where in hell were you going to find babes like that and all the beer you could drink for free?"

Thinking about the beer, Fieffer swallowed a couple of times. I swallowed too. Out on the boat deck the rear admiral, with other problems, did what he could.

The wind continued to blow hard all that night from the east. Eddie and Fieffer spelled me at the wheel, and I got a good night's sleep. It was still howling out of the east, and we were running at better than her average hull speed, almost planing down the long glassy inclines of the sea, with each frustrated comber failing to keep up with us. Ricky had found some red, gold, and black lacquer and had begun to paint a magnificent Chinese dragon under the name of the vessel on the stack. Peacock began to get itchy about our position and was shooting off his big mouth in the galley.

That curious tension between a captain who knows where he is and how to make a safe landfall and a crew that is completely dependent on him was accentuated by the anxiety of being aboard a less-than-seaworthy vessel. However, nobody paid much attention to Peacock when he verbalized his doubts.

The third day out, Fieffer was on watch and he went into the consequences of his membership in the California Bund.

"That's why the FBI started tailing me. They have tailed me for three years now. I was torpedoed in the South Pacific and spent a week on a raft before they picked me up. After we were picked up, I was brought back to San Francisco. As soon as I landed they put a tail on me. It was kind of fun, like a game. I've figured all kinds of ways to shake them. It's like I'm somebody in an old spy movie."

W. D. brought up some coffee and I handed Fieffer the wheel. He went right on talking. Keeping the tub on her feet was now automatic. The more I learned about his seagoing experiences, the more confidence I had in the guy.

"I got another ship," said Fieffer, "and I made the North Atlantic run to Murmansk. That time we were bombed. The ship went down. They fished us out of the water and took us back to New York in a destroyer. As soon as I stepped off that tin can, they started tailing me again. I generally ducked them in the subway. I did it the way they do it in the films—by sticking my foot in the door just as the train was about to pull out of the station. Sometimes there were two guys tailing me, and I had to do it twice. It was easy."

On the evening of the fourth day at sea, the heavy wind from the east that was shoving us along at a heartening pace began to moderate. We were down near the latitude of Hawaii. With no inkling of our longitude, we could not help looking out over the bow of the tug for the cumulus clouds that often gather above a body of land. It was wishful thinking. We had a long way to go.

Eddie came up on my watch that evening. The wind was

still out of the east, but it had diminished to a point that made living aboard that foolish vessel almost as nice as an ocean liner.

Eddie said, "When the Pacific is pacific, it is a nice place to be."

A sliver of moon was in the western sky. Eddie began to tell me about his life in New Orleans.

"I had a job," he said, "driving a delivery truck for a dry-cleaning outfit. I was shacked up with the most beautiful little Cajun girl you ever saw. I called her Bouncey. It was just a pet name. I really was in love with her."

Eddie was in a romantic mood. "Whatever happened to her?" I asked.

"I had a good job," Eddie went on, leaning out of the pilothouse window and watching that sliver of moon slide behind a segment of cloud and reappear. "I had a damn good salary and there were all kinds of extras. If I got a suit that didn't look too dirty and the customer wanted it dry cleaned, I would just have it steam pressed and charge him for a dry-cleaning job. I put the difference in my pocket. Bouncey and I lived high on the hog."

Eddie was quiet for a moment waiting for the sliver of moon to come out behind the cloud. "I really was crazy in love with that babe. We had a nice apartment and the money was rolling in. One day she said, 'Eddie, I want you to marry me'."

"Maybe I should have married her. Anyway I said, 'Look, my love, you are all excited. Calm down. We'll talk about it.' A few weeks went by. I kept on working. One day I came home and there were a couple of twenty-dollar bills on the bureau in the bedroom. I knew what had happened."

"What happened?"

"There was this hustler living in the next apartment who used to come over and have coffee with Bouncey."

"What did you do then, Eddie?"

"If she wanted it that way it was all right with me. I told

195

her that. I said, 'If that's the way you want it, my love, that's the way it will be.' I quit my job and tipped off all my friends who were driving hacks. She was busy as hell. I never saw so much money. I sure was wild about that babe."

Eddie was quiet now, watching the moon. Fieffer was down in the galley after a long trick at the wheel. I waited for Eddie to tell me the rest of the story while I moved the wheel a spoke or two to keep her on course. A great dark cloud moved toward the moon. The moon was lost behind it, and Eddie went on with only the light of the binnacle in the pilothouse.

"Life was pretty fancy for a while. I bought a lot of new clothes and I spent most of the day in the pool parlor while she was raking in the dough. I had it real easy. I'd come home late, have a nice dinner, and get a little on the late watch."

"You got used to it," I said.

"It wasn't hard to get used to. I had it all my own way." Eddie hesitated. "One night I came home and she was gone. I couldn't believe it. She packed her bag and blew. I was really in love with her."

It sounded like the end of the story, but it wasn't. "About two years later I ran into her. She was pushing a baby carriage. She said, 'Hello, Eddie. You know I'm married now.' She showed me her ring. 'Do you want to see the baby?' "

There was nothing more to tell. We stood there in the semidarkness. Suddenly, Eddie and I spotted two tiny lights in the sky ahead that came at us with a dazzling rapidity. It looked like a dive bomber spitting gunfire. We fell to the deck waiting for the smashing staccato of machine gun bullets.

Nothing happened. We crawled to our feet and peered over the edge of the pilothouse window. We had to laugh. Those two tiny lights in the sky that came flaming at us were the two points of the crescent moon cut off by the hard straight edge of cloud. As the cloud moved, the points grew ominously bigger. It scared the hell out of us.

Fieffer came up from the galley just when we were getting up off the deck. He wondered what in hell was going on.

The following wind remained moderate on the fifth day out. The sky was clear and the sunshine sparkled on the surface of the sea. We surprised a school of whales and watched them take off to the north, with their great flukes lifting and scooping under, and their spoutholes sending plumes of spray that curved to leeward in the gentle wind. There were some ominous cirrus clouds like mare's tails high in the sky, and a plane droned overhead and circled around us.

It was an Army Air Force plane. I thought that I might be able to get a longitude from it and I signaled. There was no reply. Evidently nobody on the plane could read code. They kept circling. I was worried that they might indicate our position to a Japanese sub, and I kept flashing, "Go away, go away."

It went away at last for reasons of its own.

Fieffer took the wheel and started talking about his problems with Military Intelligence.

"As much as they chased me when I was ashore, they never bothered me aboard ship," he said. "Not until the last trip I made. It is getting kind of nice out at sea. There haven't been many torpedoings. Last trip, though, I felt that the FBI must have said something to the old man. I could tell by the way he acted toward me. Sometimes they tell the captain of a ship. But this is only a tug. I didn't think that they would bother to tell the captain of a tug."

The wind began to pipe up again. The vessel fell behind the sea and lurched down the long shiny embankment of a swell. Fieffer handled the wheel well looking out at a comber that fanned out before us. "They didn't," he asked, "did they?"

I broke out the sextant and watched the sun still rising in

the sky. "Did they?" asked Fieffer, looking around at me while I read the vernier of the sextant through the tiny magnifying glass.

"Sure, sure," I said.

31

I had been watching the barometer, fearful of a low reading and just as wary of a high one. The mercury began to climb. The high cirrus clouds and the mare's tail in the sky gave us some idea of what to expect.

The wind from the east became more boisterous. By the sixth day it had mounted to gale proportions. The danger of a broach became so imminent that I didn't dare trust anyone at the wheel, even Fieffer. The seas that came after us from the stern were mountainous.

I said to Eddie, "I wish the guys back in the War Department could see this tub now."

Eddie had no comment. He watched the great hollows that opened before us and waited tensely as the following crest broke along the bulwarks and gave us a violent pitch forward. I had slowed the engine. We had steerage and the wind and the sea moved us like a sailing vessel plummeting wing and wing downwind.

By sundown the dry gale blew itself out. I gave her "Full Ahead," and the mountains of water behind us no longer crested. Fieffer took the wheel and I put the earphones on and began to listen through the static for some sign of life, a living voice from Hawaii. We had to be getting near the place.

I heard a voice. I heard a reply. Two vessels were speaking to each other. One guy said, "I'll give you a time tick. When you hear the sound it will be exactly 1:43 GMT."

While I waited for the sound I set my wristwatch to 1:42, and when the sound came I put the minute hand right on 43 and made a mental note of the position of the secondhand on my watch.

I had Greenwich Mean Time. Now I could find our longitude and calculate our time of arrival. I could hardly wait for the stars to come out.

As the night deepened, one by one the stars took their places in the sky. The moon was fatter now, and from the top of a long swell I could see a shining white line thrown by the moon along the horizon. The three stars that form the belt of Orion, the hunter, pointed at the unmistakable Dog Star, Sirius. It was the brightest star in the sky. I brought it down with the sextant and swung it like a pendulum until it grazed the line of light on the horizon. Then I looked at my watch.

I did it the hard way, changing the Greenwich time to sidereal time and using the tables in Bowdich to solve the astronomical triangles. We had none of the line-of-position tables on board. I explained the process to Kidd, who stood beside me at the chart table and corrected a couple of errors. It took almost an hour.

We plotted our longitude on the chart and crossed it with the latitude we had found at noon. The ST250 was bound to raise the lighthouse on Molokai on the fourth day of the fourth month of 1944. It was nice to know where we were.

Kidd went down into the galley. Peacock was down there. Kidd tried to tell him. The chief didn't believe him.

32

The rancorous surf that had catapulted us westward evened out at dawn. Ricky was on the starboard boat deck with a can of gold lacquer, putting the finishing touches on the Chinese dragon that adorned the stack. Ralph was hanging on the boat-deck rail waiting for the final heave that would turn him inside out. His glassy eyes were contemplating the curl of surf as the blunt bow of the ST250 sliced the mirror of the sea. It was the only white water in the vast expanse of bottle blue that reached out to a string of cumulus clouds along the western sky. Peacock had the engine spinning down below, and we were moving at better than nine knots. The longitude I had gotten from that lucky shot of the Dog Star and with the help of Kidd, who had corrected a couple of errors in addition, put us exactly 120 miles from the longitude of Honolulu.

As I came out into the pilothouse, Peacock came up on deck and sat on the cruciform bit on the fo'c'slehead with a cigarette dangling from his lower lip.

I had just gotten up out of the lower bunk, fitted my truss into place, and pulled my pants on. It had become too warm to wear a shirt. I lit a cigarette and stared down at Peacock. He had that characteristic sneer on his face.

"Do you know where the hell you are?" he asked.

"Yeah," I said, "I know exactly where the hell I am."

"Where the hell are you?"

"I am exactly 120 miles from Honolulu and you are damn lucky that you are not in irons."

"You missed the Hawaiian Islands altogether and you're heading for Japan."

"Peacock, my fine feathered friend, you are as full of crap as a Christmas turkey."

Somebody laughed. Peacock got up, flipped his butt over the side and walked toward the engine room door. He passed just below Ralph and ducked below just as the poor bastard came up with one tremendous dry heave.

Ralph sucked air. There was a prolonged rattle in his throat. His eyes bulged and turned slightly aft to focus on something in the water that took him back to happier days in California, when he went fishing with his father. It reminded him of the ripple made by a number-three spoon in the magic waters of Baja California. It brought back lovely recollections of the same lure in Lake Tahoe and the wonderful world of rich kids.

The ripple in the water grew in size as he stared at it. A funny-looking metallic thing broke the surface where the ripple had been. When it lifted still further and swung a shiny eye in his direction, Ralph froze. Suddenly, as if by some strange alchemy, the spasms of regurgitation ceased. His vertigo vanished. In the wild appraisal of the situation, Ralph straightened up and stared vacantly about him. He walked to the window of the pilothouse, the color suddenly back in his face, the blood in his temples pulsating.

I looked at him in disbelief, reached down to where his hat with the omelet on the visor hung on the window crank. I slammed it on his head, and said, "Admiral, I'm glad to see you back among the living."

The visor of his cap hung down obscuring his eyes. The gold filigree of the omelet floated slowly up as he lifted his head and tried to peer beneath the rim, while his left hand lifted and pointed aft.

I followed the line of his arm to a spot just aft of us in the sea, where the periscope of a submarine was throwing a rapidly expanding wake as it grew into a great black conning tower. The sub had surfaced.

There was a whirring sound, a click and slam, and before I could run and get the .45 that lay in my cabin drawer, the commander of the submarine was in the conning tower, and a Japanese marine with a machine gun was making practice passes at us from a platform on the long narrow deck.

We were caught flat-footed. Our machine guns were in the bilge doing double duty as ballast.

A bullhorn spoke, "Stop engine."

There was no way to turn and ram. My .45 was useless. I rang the telegraph, "stop."

Peacock came running up on deck. I heard him say, "Jesus Christ, we are in Jap territory."

Now the reverberating voice of the bullhorn said, "All on deck."

Ricky laid down his brush after wiping it with a rag and deliberately pounded close the cover of the gold paint with his heel. The two other engineers came up out of the engine room. W. D., the cook, came out of the galley with a pot in one hand and his eyes hanging out of his head.

There was some very efficient scurrying about on the submarine as the ST250, her engine silent, slowly drifted ahead. A rubber dinghy appeared and was seen being launched over the side. A heaving line with a grappling hook at the end of it came whizzing over to put the bite on our bulwark forward. Four men, two with machine pistols and two with sidearms, were seen getting into the dinghy and pulling themselves the forty feet that separated us.

They came aboard like gorillas, one climbing the port

ladder in two leaps and the other going down below, while the remaining two swung around the deck flinging open every cabin door. We were ordered to line up on the boat deck aft.

Another boatload of officers came aboard in another rubber boat. As we stood on the afterdeck I could hear the crack of rifle butts on the wireless equipment and the staccato of machine pistol bullets that was employed to finish the job. A Japanese officer, who was probably the second in command, was seen shoving Ralph toward the after boat deck. Ralph had been standing transfixed with his back to the sea and his fists glued to the steel railing.

"You captain?" asked the man from the submarine, confronting Ralph and pointing to the omelet on his cap.

Ralph looked at him as the full impact of his vanity in acquiring that coveted symbol of authority slowly swept over him. The officer pulled his sidearm and pointed it threateningly at his face. "You captain?" he asked.

Ralph stared. His jaw dropped and his body, so long without nourishment, began to quake and tremble. The officer jerked the pin of the hand gun back into firing position. "You captain?" he shrieked.

I spoke up. "I am the captain."

The interrogator unleashed his fury on me. "You captain?"

"Yes," I said, "I am the captain."

One of the rubber dinghys had been pulled back to its mother ship and the commander came aboard. He had a pleasant face and I could see how the prestige of authority had lent to him a certain geniality. The interrogator continued his technique of harassment. Turning to the rest of the crew and pointing to me with the hand gun he asked, "He captain?"

There was a chorus of assent from the crew. When a man who seemed from the insignia on his sleeve to be the commander of the submarine came up on the boat deck, there was a short conversation in Japanese and the commander faced me in a friendly manner.

He had felt the vessel heel slightly when he stepped foot on her. His eye, practiced in the subtle balance of a submarine, surveyed the ST250. "Captain," he said, "Where you come from?"

"New Orleans," I said.

A faint smile played across his features. "Where?" he asked.

"New Orleans," I repeated.   •

His slanted eyes opened wide, and a slight rumble of risibility began to rock his frame. He wagged his head.

"New Orleans," he said, "in this?"

"Yes," I said.

He shook his head looking up at the steel pilothouse, the steel mast, the massive steel structure of the whole upper deck. His shoulders rocked from side to side and a sceptical smile settled on his round face.

I waited. He controlled his mirth and then he pointed to the submarine that lay off our port quarter and then down at the ST250. He held up two fingers in a travesty on the V-for-victory symbol.

I got the drift. He and I were masters of two different kinds of death traps. "Yesterday very bad storm," he said.

"Yes, very bad storm."

The second in command of the sub had my men lined up along the boat deck railing, and one of the Japanese sailors was frisking them. When it came my turn, the second in command did the job. When he felt the steel band that held the pad of the truss in place, he jumped back and pointed the muzzle of his machine pistol in my face.

A few excited words in Japanese indicated that I was packing a hand gun. The commander waved him aside. Then to me he made a gesture of unbuckling his belt. The implication was clear.

I followed instructions. My pants fell to my knees. When the commander saw the shiny metal spring holding the pad of the truss, the smile left his face and he appeared quite solemn.

He took one step toward me, made a gentle bow and sharply ordered his men back to the submarine. We saw them jettison our machine guns over the side and tote the last carton of cigarettes with them as they paddled back to the submarine.

The commander was the last to leave the tug. Before he stepped into the rubber dinghy he pointed westward, and with a gesture that could almost have been taken for a salute, he said, "You steer Honolulu."

Peacock who had been growling about missing the Hawaiian Islands altogether and winding up in Japanese territory began to see the light. He jumped down below and started up the engine. I pulled up my pants, winked at the crew, and said, "Let's go."

We took off with the submarine still on the surface and

keeping up with us right off our port quarter. Their five-inch gun had been unlimbered, and the barrel of that wicked-looking job was trained right on our pilothouse.

Now Ralph, who had taken some nourishment, came up the ladder to the pilothouse and demanded the right to go to work. I put him at the wheel. He steered a fair course.

West was 270 on the compass. We were headed 269, which added up to 17, which in turn added up to 8. It was as close to west as I could steer without putting a jinx on the vessel.

The sky was clear. Both vessels moved as if on glass. It became midday. Eddie and Kidd went below to grab a bite and I got a shot of the sun for a meridian altitude. After I plotted our latitude on the chart, I found that the current, which had befriended us all the way across, had shoved us ten miles too far north. I said to Ralph, over my shoulder, "Swing her over to southeast."

Ralph turned around and asked, "Why?"

It was a perfectly innocent question. It was the kind of an innocent question, which asked at sea of a superior officer, can get your head handed to you.

I looked at my knuckles, and I thought about all the tough Nova Scotian mates and all the hard-case captains that would have crippled this guy for asking a question like that. The only proper punishment I could think of was to encourage that kind of arrogance. One day the right disciplinarian would come along and this punk would be taught a lesson.

"That's right, Ralph," I said, "Always ask the captain or the mate why when he gives you an order. It is a fine way of showing that you possess what is known as intellectual curiosity. Or else, you have been listening to that crazy chief engineer. Now, goddamn it, put her head on 224."

He swung the vessel to port and the submarine swung with us like soldiers parading "squads left" as we approached the Hawaiian Islands.

33

With a generous assist from the North Equatorial Current, which the Navy had never heard about or chose to ignore, the ST250, with a Japanese submarine using her for a radar shield, was rapidly approaching the Hawaiian Islands. They tailed us like the FBI tailed Fieffer. On the eighth day, after tailing us for twenty-four hours, the submarine suddenly submerged.

Except for the wreckage of the radio gear in the pilot-house, the loss of the machine guns and the cigarettes they had appropriated, we were in good shape. We were now less than two hundred miles from the lighthouse on Molokai. It would show up at four o'clock in the morning of the ninth day.

It did. About a half hour before it showed, we saw a loom of light along the horizon dead ahead. At five minutes after four it blossomed into a blessed blink.

Due to the presence of the submarine and the general anxiety, I hadn't hit the sack for more than twenty-four hours. When the light on Molokai materialized and we made a positive identification, I gave Eddie a coastwise course into Honolulu Harbor and collapsed.

I missed the majesty of the great, black, bulbous volcanic cliffs, with the early morning sun glancing across them. I missed the excitement of that coastwise run, with the mountains on the left and the sea as blue as the color on the national emblem and the sight of the rolling white surf along the black volcanic sand of the beaches.

Ricky described it to me when I woke at the dock in Honolulu Harbor. A Coast Guard officer had come down when Eddie brought the ST250 alongside some pilings. Eddie rigged a plank from the pilings to the tug for a passage ashore. The Coast Guard officer was a great barrel of a man. "How am I supposed to come aboard?" he asked Eddie.

"You walk the plank just like we do,' said Eddie.

The Coast Guard inspector contemplated the narrow bridge. It was six inches wide. "Is your captain on board?"

"He's on board," said Eddie.

"Well, get him out here."

"He's asleep." Then in explanation, "He hasn't had any sleep for twenty-four hours."

"Get him out here."

"You can go to hell," said Eddie.

"I'll take his license away from him," he threatened.

"Fat chance," said Eddie, "he hasn't got any goddamn license."

The Coast Guard officer waddled away, frothing at the mouth.

Around noon, I struggled out of my bunk and Eddie told me about his conversation with the man from the Coast Guard. It was about time I reported to the Navy office. I walked the plank and stopped to ask about the ST249 at the dockmaster's office. Our companion vessel had not arrived. I wondered if she ever would and whether Dyer had succumbed to the Navy sailing orders.

At the Navy building I inquired for the Navy commander to whom I was supposed to report our arrival. I found him quite amenable. A pretty WAVE brought me a cup of coffee.

I presented my sailing orders without comment, and I took a seat across from him at his desk. "We were boarded by a Japanese submarine," I said.

"Yes, we know," said the Navy commander. "We spotted him. But don't worry about it, son. I think we got him."

"You got him?"

"Yes, we got him."

"That's too bad," I said, "he was a nice guy."

AFT

The crew of the ST250 monkeyed around the Island of Oahu for three weeks. Ten days after we arrived in Honolulu Harbor the ST249 showed up. Dyer had finally abandoned the great circle course given him by the Navy and wandered a couple of hundred miles south of the latitude of Hawaii. He backtracked and guessed his way around for twenty days. The crew was on short rations and the vessel was damn near out of fuel. The crew was at the breaking point.

At last, in desperation, Dyer opened up with his radio. The Coast Guard picked up the signal and found him wallowing around far south of Hilo. They escorted him into the harbor of Honolulu.

I had met a lot of Hawaiians and they were a sweet people. I was offered a job running the ST250 around the islands. Most of the local pilots were Hawaiians. I turned the job down. I didn't want to take the job away from one of the local boys.

At last we were given passage to San Francisco on a troop transport. All the way across the Pacific, until we landed in San Francisco, Dyer, who had a bunk next to mine, kept

211

sharpening a switchblade knife on the sole of his shoe and staring at me.

We boarded a train for Los Angeles. Waiting for another train that would take us back to New Orleans, I made a special trip to Wilmington. I headed for the office of the colonel in charge of Military Intelligence.

When I walked in I said, "You've got to stop hounding that fellow you thought was a spy."

"You mean Fieffer, the boy we asked you to watch?"

"That's right," I said, "The guy has done enough for his country. He is a loyal American and he is a sailor."

"Thanks," said the colonel. "That's all we wanted to know."

"By the way, don't you think you could spare a promotion for him?"

The colonel shook his head in the negative. "I believe that there is a promotion in line for the other boy."

"You mean the one with the omelet on his visor?"

"That's the one. The boy with the gold braid on his cap."

Despite the triumphant windup in our battle with the sea, I walked out of the colonel's office with a vague sense of defeat.

Back in New Orleans there were more small tugs to deliver just as tender as the ST250. I was getting ready to take one with a massive barge up to New York when the major in charge took the sextant off my vessel.

I raised holy hell about it. The major said, "You don't need that sextant. You can buoy-hop all the way up the coast."

"I suppose you think that I buoy-hopped all the way to Honolulu?"

There was an older guy standing with the major when I spoke. He tried to approach me. The major kept dragging him away.

He broke loose at last and came over to speak to me. "Did

I hear you say that you took one of these small tugs to Hawaii?"

"That's right," I said.

"I am with the War Department," he said by way of introduction. "I am in charge of this operation."

"How do you do," I said.

"Tell me," he said, "how did you do it?"

"Do what?"

"Get her across the Pacific?"

It would have seemed tedious and irrelevant to go into detail, my background in sailboats, my affair with *Princess,* the admonition I had received from Captain Erbe, the casual conversation I had with a shellback in Newport Beach, the jettison of superfluous government property, and my contempt for Navy sailing orders.

"Why do you ask?" I said.

The man from the War Department hesitated. "Go ahead," I said, "you can't hurt my feelings."

"We lost so many," he said.

That was the end of ocean passages in small tugs. The War Department found more interesting ways to capsize them and dispatch their crews to a wet hereafter. They turned them over to the Navy, which proceeded to tow them across the Atlantic Ocean for the invasion at D-day, with a record of losing every one en route.

In the brief interlude between voyages, I ran into Colonel Rogers, who was chief of staff at the Port of Embarkation in New Orleans. I hadn't seen him since my one-man show and before I delivered the ST250 to Honolulu. He shook my hand and said, "Glad to see you back." Then, as he turned to walk away, he hesitated, shook my hand again, and said, "We won't do that to you again."